NOW YOU DON'T . . .

"Now we've got him," Jacob snarled.

Not if Fargo could help it. Rather than be overwhelmed, he went at them, hitting hard, hitting fast, first one man and then another. In their drunken state they were sluggish. It cost them. He bloodied a mouth, rammed his fist into an eye, split an ear. A knee arced at his manhood. Sidestepping, he planted the toe of his boot between Jacob's legs. The man with the busted nose lunged, seeking to wrap his bony fingers around his neck; Fargo gave him a straight arm to the face that felled him where he stood.

Only one of the drunks was still on his feet and he was the fastest. He slipped a cross that should have laid him out and retaliated with short blows thrown at Fargo's eyes. Tucking at the knees, Fargo rammed his fist up under the man's sternum. He folded in on himself and lay in a heap. . . .

THE TRAILSMAN

#367

TEXAS
TEMPEST

by

Jon Sharpe

A SIGNET BOOK

SIGNET
Published by New American Library, a division of
Penguin Group (USA) Inc., 375 Hudson Street,
New York, New York 10014, USA
Penguin Group (Canada), 90 Eglinton Avenue East, Suite 700, Toronto,
Ontario M4P 2Y3, Canada (a division of Pearson Penguin Canada Inc.)
Penguin Books Ltd., 80 Strand, London WC2R 0RL, England
Penguin Ireland, 25 St. Stephen's Green, Dublin 2,
Ireland (a division of Penguin Books Ltd.)
Penguin Group (Australia), 250 Camberwell Road, Camberwell, Victoria 3124,
Australia (a division of Pearson Australia Group Pty. Ltd.)
Penguin Books India Pvt. Ltd., 11 Community Centre, Panchsheel Park,
New Delhi - 110 017, India
Penguin Group (NZ), 67 Apollo Drive, Rosedale, Auckland 0632,
New Zealand (a division of Pearson New Zealand Ltd.)
Penguin Books (South Africa) (Pty.) Ltd., 24 Sturdee Avenue,
Rosebank, Johannesburg 2196, South Africa

Penguin Books Ltd., Registered Offices:
80 Strand, London WC2R 0RL, England

First published by Signet, an imprint of New American Library,
a division of Penguin Group (USA) Inc.

First Printing, May 2012
10   9   8   7   6   5   4   3   2   1

The first chapter of this book previously appeared in *Mountains of No Return*, the
three hundred sixty-sixth volume in this series.

The Trailsman

Beginnings . . . they bend the tree and they mark the man. Skye Fargo was born when he was eighteen. Terror was his midwife, vengeance his first cry. Killing spawned Skye Fargo, ruthless, cold-blooded murder. Out of the acrid smoke of gunpowder still hanging in the air, he rose, cried out a promise never forgotten.

The Trailsman they began to call him all across the West: searcher, scout, hunter, the man who could see where others only looked, his skills for hire but not his soul, the man who lived each day to the fullest, yet trailed each tomorrow. Skye Fargo, the Trailsman, the seeker who could take the wildness of a land and the wanting of a woman and make them his own.

The wilds of West Texas, 1861—
where certain death waited for the unwary.

The fight just sort of happened.

Skye Fargo was at the bar of the Zachary Saloon when one of three rowdy men next to him bumped his arm. He was jostled so hard, whiskey spilled over his chin and down his shirt. He glared at the man, but the three ignored him. They were drunk, and laughing and joking and pushing one another.

Fargo's temper flared. A big man, broad of shoulder and narrow at the waist, he wore buckskins and a red bandanna, and a Colt high on his hip. He set down his glass and swore.

The three had polished off a bottle and were working on the second. By their clothes they were laborers, several of the many workers on the new buildings going up. Corpus Christi, Texas, was growing by the proverbial leaps and bounds.

"Watch what you're doing, you jackass," Fargo growled, and motioned at the bartender for a refill.

The man who had jostled him turned. He was a block of muscle with a square chin covered with stubble. "Were you talkin' to me?"

Fargo gestured at the wet stain on his shirt and wiped his dripping chin with his sleeve. "I sure as hell am."

"What did I do?"

"Are you blind? You made me spill my drink." Fargo figured that was the end of it and faced the bar. He was wrong. The man poked his shoulder.

"Don't talk to me like that and then turn away. I don't like it."

"I don't give a good damn what you like," Fargo told him.

The man placed his big hands on his hips and puffed out his chest. "You hear this bastard, boys? Sayin' I pushed him."

The other two moved closer to their friend. One had beetling brows and the other a crooked nose.

"Even if you did, Jacob, he had no call to insult you," Beetling Brows said.

Crooked Nose nodded. "You ask me, he should apologize."

"You hear that?" Jacob said to Fargo. "Say you're sorry."

"Like hell," Fargo said. "You bumped me. I didn't bump you."

"You called me a jackass."

"I take it back."

"You do?"

Fargo nodded. He knew he shouldn't say what he was about to, but he couldn't help himself. "You're a dumb son of a bitch who doesn't know when to leave well enough be."

A flush spread up Jacob's face. "Is that so?" he grated.

"I think you should buy me a drink to make up for the one you made me spill."

"Is that so?" Jacob said again, and glanced at his companions. "Do you want to know what I think?" He didn't wait for them to answer. "I think we should pound this gent into the floor."

"Maybe break a few bones while we're at it," Beetling Brows said.

"And then throw him out back with the trash," Crooked Nose chimed in.

Jacob smiled and smacked his right fist into his left palm. "Who wants to start the fun?"

"I do," Fargo said, and unleashed an uppercut that tilted Jacob onto his heels. A left hook sent him crashing onto a table.

For a few seconds the other two were rooted in stunned disbelief, which was all the opening Fargo needed to wade in and let fly with a flurry of jabs that drove both men stumbling back. He slammed a solid right to Beetling Brow's jaw, spun, and drove his left fist deep into Crooked Nose's gut.

All three were down, but they didn't stay there. Bellowing like a mad bull, Jacob heaved to his feet and lumbered at Fargo with his fists cocked. The bartender yelled something about not damaging the place. Fargo ducked an awkward looping right, delivered a powerful left, evaded another swing, and connected with a knuckle-buster to the chin.

Jacob crashed down a second time.

The others were rising. Boiling fury blazed in their eyes.

Fargo didn't let them set themselves. He was on them in a

whirlwind of blows, his arms like steam-engine pistons. He broke the crooked nose and pulped the beetling brow.

Fargo's right hand hurt like hell, but he ignored the pain. He stood over the three, poised to tear into them again should it be necessary. "No more," he warned. "Let it drop."

The other patrons had stopped what they were doing to gape. Fistfights weren't all that common. Most Texans settled disputes with their six-shooters.

Out in the street a wagon clattered.

Jacob slowly sat up. He rubbed his jaw and looked at his friends and they looked at him and all three nodded.

"Hell," Fargo said.

In unison they came up and simultaneously attacked.

Fargo blocked, countered, gave way. He'd been in more than his share of barroom brawls, but three at once were too many and some of their punches slipped through. His left cheek exploded in pain. His temple was clipped. A boot arced at his groin and he narrowly avoided it. He kept on retreating and then suddenly he was against a wall and they had him half-ringed.

"Now we've got him," Jacob snarled.

Not if Fargo could help it. Rather than be overwhelmed, he went at them, hitting hard, hitting fast, first one man and then another. In their drunken state they were sluggish. It cost them. He bloodied a mouth, rammed his fist into an eye, split an ear. A knee arced at his manhood. Sidestepping, he planted the toe of his boot between Jacob's legs. The man with the busted nose lunged, seeking to wrap his bony fingers around his neck; Fargo gave him a straight arm to the face that felled him where he stood.

Only one of the drunks was still on his feet and he was the fastest. He slipped a cross that should have laid him out and retaliated with short blows thrown at Fargo's eyes. Tucking at the knees, Fargo rammed his fist up under the man's sternum. Beetling Brow folded in on himself and lay in a heap.

Fargo was breathing heavily. His temple was sore and his ribs were hurting. He waited for them to resume the fight, but all three stayed on the floor. Realizing it was over, he went to the bar and gulped the refill.

"That was some fist-slingin'," the bartender said by way of praise.

Fargo tapped the glass. "Another."

"Serves them right," the bartender said as he took a bottle from a shelf. "But you might want to skedaddle in case the sheriff shows up."

Fargo didn't see how the sheriff could blame him for any of it, but he had somewhere to be, anyway, so he nodded, drained the glass, and paid.

"Come again," the bartender said.

Corpus Christi had grown since Fargo was there last. About twenty years ago, there had been nothing but a trading post. Then a few settlers moved in, and the army came and stayed awhile, and before long a small town sprang up. Thanks to the bay, ships were constantly coming and going. With the commerce came prosperity and that lured more people. Now Corpus Christi was well on its way to becoming a full-fledged city.

The ship Fargo was looking for was out of France. It was called the *Relaise*. She was a four-master, a clipper out of Marseille. Two hundred and fifty feet long, she carried both passengers and cargo.

Finding her was easy. She was the only four-master at dock.

A sailor in a cap stopped Fargo at the bottom of the gangway. "That is far enough, monsieur," he politely said in a heavy accent. "State your business, *s'il vous plaît*."

"I'm here to see the count," Fargo said. "He sent for me."

The sailor snapped straight and said, "Comte Louis Tristan of Valois?"

"That's his handle, if *comte* means count," Fargo said.

"*Un* moment," the sailor said. "I will be right back." And with that he hastened up the gangway.

Fargo hooked his thumbs in his gun belt. He didn't mind waiting. The count had sent him two hundred dollars as an advance against possible employment, so he'd hear the man out.

The sky was a vivid blue broken by a few puffy clouds. Gulls wheeled and squawked. The wind had momentarily stilled and the surface of the bay was a sheet of glass.

Fargo liked the sea but not nearly as much as the prairie and the mountains. Endless water wasn't the same as endless grass and neither could hold a candle to peaks that towered miles above the earth. He'd taken a voyage to Hawaii once, and that was enough of the ocean to last him a lifetime.

Feet pattered on the deck above and two figures appeared at the top of the gangway. Both took one look at him and put their hands over their mouths and giggled.

"Lord Almighty," Fargo breathed.

They were twins, nearly identical in every respect, with golden curls and eyes as blue as the sky. High cheekbones, delectable lips, and cantaloupes for bosoms added to their allure. Holding hands, they grinned coquettishly and sashayed down. Both were dressed in the height of European fashion, in sweeping dresses and hats that only females could love.

Fargo doffed his and said simply, "Ladies." If he had to guess, he'd peg their age at twenty or so.

They did more giggling and studied him openly from head to toe.

"*Très beau*, eh?" the twin on the right said.

"*Magnifique*," said the other.

The first one whispered in the ear of the second and both grinned like cats about to devour a canary.

"I'm Fargo," Fargo introduced himself. "I'm waiting on Count Louis. Could be you know him?"

"*Oui*, monsieur," said the twin on the left, giving a little curtsey.

"We know him quite well," said the other in English. "Better than most anyone except perhaps *notre mère*."

"Our mama," said the gorgeous vision on the left.

"Don't tell me," Fargo said.

"*Oui*," the twin on the right said.

"We are his daughters."

Fargo looked from one to the other and felt a stirring, down low. He hadn't heard what the job was yet, but he'd already made up his mind.

He would take it.

2

The ship's stateroom, as they called it, was the most spacious on the vessel. It had all the comforts of home if the home was a palace. Carpet on the floor, brass everywhere, and a large mahogany table were a testament to the elegance.

Fargo sat at one end of the table with his hat in front of him and reminded himself that he'd tangled with Apaches and the Sioux and some of the worst bad men west of the Mississippi. He could take a little scrutiny.

Only this was more than a little. Eight people were studying him as if he were an unknown sea creature pulled out of the bay in a net.

At the other end of the table sat Count Louis Tristan of Valois. He was short and portly and not anything at all like Fargo had imagined a count would be. But he dressed the part, with a jacket and matching pants and a ruffled shirt and a wide belt with a buckle big enough to use to beat a snake to death. He had nice teeth, which he flashed a lot.

"I am grateful you came, Monsieur Fargo," he was saying with an accent, and waved his fingers as he spoke. "I was told you can be depended upon and you have proven it to be true."

"What's this about a job?" Fargo said. "I spent most of the two hundred on booze and cards."

The count blinked and laughed, and when he laughed, so did everyone else.

"It is all about money with you, then?" Louis said.

"Hell," Fargo said. "I spend it as quick as I make it. If I like a job, I take it. If I don't, I won't. The money doesn't matter much."

"Interesting," Louis said. "But I have been remiss. Permit me to introduce my family. As their lives will be in your hands, they get to have a say in whether we hire your services." He indicated a woman on his right. "May I present the Comtessa Henriette Tristan, my wife. The countess and I have been married twenty-seven years, and all of them bliss."

Fargo saw where the twins got their looks. Henriette Tristan was a head-turner. She had the same golden curls and blue eyes, and for a woman who must be past forty, she made him think of a ripe cherry that begged to be plucked from the tree. "How do you do, ma'am?"

"Monsieur," Henriette said in a sultry purr.

"And these," Louis said, nodding at the twins on his left, "are my daughters. You've already met them."

"They never said their names."

Louis frowned and clucked at the pair of beauties. "Where are your manners? This one"—and he pointed—"is Blanche. She is older by two minutes. This other one"—and he pointed—"is Jeanne."

"I can't tell one from the other," Fargo admitted.

"There are ways, monsieur," Jeanne said with an impish grin.

Louis pointed at two young men. One was short like him and the other tall like Henriette. "These are my sons."

The short one was named Philip and the one who took after their mother was Charles.

"I am most pleased to meet you, monsieur," Philip said eagerly. "I have read much about frontier scouts. The many perils you face. Perils from the red man, yes? And from wild beasts? From raging floods and the burning sun. It is most exciting, *non*?"

"If you call drowning exciting," Fargo said.

Philip acted confused and then said, "Ah. I see. You poke fun at me. But in *The Dastardly Deeds of Desperado Dan*, I read where—"

"*Stupide*." Charles cut him off. He seemed bored. "You and those silly stories."

"But I am right, am I not?" Philip appealed to Fargo. "There are savages and beasts and all the rest?"

"Out in the wilds," Fargo said, "you never know if you'll make it through the day."

"See?" Philip said to his brother.

"Oh, please," Charles replied.

Count Tristan cleared his throat. "That will be enough. We

7

don't want to give the wrong impression." He motioned at the last couple, a middle-aged man and woman.

The man's features reminded Fargo of a hawk. "And this is my wife's sister, Odette, and her husband and good friend of mine, Claude Dupree."

"How do you do, monsieur?" Claude said. He sat stiffly in his chair, his hands clasped in front of him. "My brother-in-law has spoken most highly of you."

"How can he?" Fargo said. "We've never met."

"Ah," Count Tristan said, and beamed. "I have friends in high places. One of them is Senator Lane. He put me in touch with some high-ranking officers in your military. I put the same question to each of them, and their answer was always the same."

"What question?"

"I told them that I desired to take my family on an excursion into your great West and that it behooves me to hire the best guide that money can buy." Louis beamed. "All of them had the highest praise for you."

"There are other good scouts—" Fargo began.

"True. Each officer did, in fact, provide a short list. But one name and one name only was on each. So I sent the two hundred dollars and requested your presence, and here you are." Louis summed up his account.

Fargo debated with himself. He supposed he could take them to the prairie country up around the Platte River. It should be safe enough. There were few hostiles and plenty of game. They might even get in a buffalo hunt.

Count Tristan had gone on with "I can see you hesitate, but I assure you I have this planned down to the smallest detail. As an inducement, I'm willing to pay you five thousand American dollars."

Fargo sat up. "How much?"

"You heard me correctly, monsieur. Five thousand dollars for a few weeks of your time. We can be ready to depart by noon tomorrow if you agree."

"Not so fast," Fargo said. "It's a long ride to the Platte River country and—"

"The Platte River?" Louis said. "*Non,* monsieur. I have read of it and it is very tame. I prefer something more adventurous. It is why we came to Texas, after all."

"You already picked out where you want to go?"

"*Oui*," the count said, nodding. "And you will be happy to hear. It is much nearer than the Platte." He paused. "I would like to take a tour of west Texas."

Fargo stared.

"Is there a problem, monsieur?"

At that moment a servant that Louis had sent for coffee earlier returned and set a china cup and saucer in front of Fargo. She wore a maid's uniform that by American standards would be considered scandalous. Fargo liked it a lot. He liked the coffee, too. He sipped and pondered how best to respond. He could use the five thousand, but he wouldn't take it at the expense of their lives.

"Monsieur?" Louis prompted.

"West Texas," Fargo began, "is about as dangerous a place as you could go."

"How so?" Henriette asked.

"There are Comanches, for one thing," Fargo said. "And they hate whites for taking over land they used to roam. They won't care that you're from another country. They'll kill you as dead as they would an American."

"We will have a large party, monsieur," Louis said, "with many guns. Surely that will keep the primitives at bay."

"There's nothing primitive about the Comanches," Fargo said.

"I beg to differ, monsieur. They live in tents made of animal hides, do they not? And they use bows and arrows instead of guns."

"A Comanche warrior can let his arrows fly faster than you can shoot." Fargo set him straight. "They're the best horsemen anywhere and can ride rings around anyone in your party."

Claude Dupree sniffed and said, "I would like to see them try. I am a superb horseman."

"What else, monsieur?" Louis asked.

Fargo considered how to explain. A lot of east Texas had been settled, but the western part of the state was largely untamed. It was a wild land of hostiles and bad men and Nature at its worst. He could rattle off a list of dangers as long as his arm, but he settled for "You go out there, there's a good chance a lot of you won't make it back."

"You are attempting to frighten us," Henriette said.

"Perhaps it is a ploy to demand more money, Mother," Charles, the oldest son, suggested.

Fargo had taken an instant dislike to him, and his dislike deepened. "It's the truth, you dumb bastard. I've been there. I know."

Coloring, Charles started to rise out of his chair. "What did you call me?"

"Sit down," Louis demanded, and when his son complied, he smiled and spread his hands. "I must ask you, Monsieur Fargo, not to be so insulting. My son was only offering his opinion."

"I'm not saying all this to get more money," Fargo said. "I'm trying to warn you, but you're not listening." He leaned forward. "The Kiowa Apaches roam west Texas and they're not any friendlier than the Comanches. We run into either, it could be more trouble than we can handle. There are Comancheros in west Texas, too. They like to steal white women and horses and guns and sell them to the Indians. Then there are the outlaws, the robbers and the killers who hide out there and prey on parties like yours. I could go on, but that should be enough."

"Most excellent," the count said, and smiled happily.

Fargo was beginning to wonder if the man was loco. "What the hell is excellent about it?"

"Please, monsieur, your language in front of the women," Louis scolded. Sitting back, he took a swallow of water, and the maid immediately refilled the glass. "Perhaps I should explain."

Fargo waited.

"I agree that the Platte River country and other regions are safer," Louis said. "But we didn't come to be safe. We get enough of safe in France. Shall I tell you how I spend my days? I spend them in dealing with matters related to my estates, or in business meetings, and at night I attend social functions commensurate with my station."

Fargo wondered what in hell *commensurate* meant.

"Need I stress how *safe* all that is? How boring? How very, very dull?" Louis shifted and drummed his fingers. "I am tired of safe, monsieur. I am tired of dull. I crave some excitement. Something different. Something to fill me with a zest for life I very much fear that I've lost."

"So you drag your family off to one of the most dangerous places anywhere?" Fargo said.

"Oh, you misconstrue, monsieur," the count said. "This wasn't my idea at all. I would have been content with a tour of the Mediterranean or Asia."

"Then who was the jackass who came up with it?" Fargo wanted to know.

Henriette Tristan smiled. "That would be me."

3

A strained silence fell. The count did more shifting in his chair. The twins and their brothers became statues. Claude's face became hard with resentment while Odette stared at her lap.

Henriette, smiling serenely, said, "So it is your opinion, Monsieur Fargo, that I shouldn't have suggested coming here to my husband?"

"You're an idiot, lady," Fargo said.

It was Claude, not the count, who pushed to his feet and balled his fists. "That will be quite enough."

"Claude, please," Odette said.

"*Non,*" Claude snapped. "Henriette is your sister. I will not stand to have her insulted." He placed his fists on the table and bent toward Fargo. "Do so again and I shall thrash you."

"Claude," Henriette said sharply, "control yourself and take your seat."

Claude scowled at Fargo but gave a slight bow to her and sank back down.

For all of a minute Fargo could have heard a pin drop.

Finally Henriette coughed. "Perhaps I should explain myself, monsieur. It might change your opinion of me." She delicately nipped her lower lip. "A few years ago I became aware that my husband has been most unhappy. He likes the outdoors. To hunt. To fish. To ride for hours. When he was younger he spent every day out and about, indulging his passion. Then he met me."

"Henriette," the count said, "that is hardly the way to express it."

"Bear with me," Henriette replied, and continued. "He loves me dearly. And because of that love, he gave up his other great love, the outdoors. He devoted himself to family matters and to business and to all the things his station requires. And little by little it ate at him until I could plainly see that he was miserable."

"I do what I have to," Louis declared.

"Do you see?" Henriette said to Fargo. "Such is his devotion to us that he has given up his other passion. But I would not have that. I would see him happy again. I would like for him to have great adventures that will stir his passion."

Fargo saw a certain logic in her thinking, but he still had to say, "Why in the world did you pick Texas, of all places?"

"Because of the many tales we heard about it," Henriette said. "You have just confirmed them by saying how dangerous it is."

"And you *want* that?" Fargo said.

"Did you not tell us that a journey to the Platte River country would be peaceful?" Henriette didn't give him a chance to answer. "Where is the adventure in that? My Louis needs excitement. The kind only Texas can provide."

"Lady," Fargo said, "he can do all the hunting and fishing he wants up along the Platte or any of a dozen other rivers."

"But don't you see? That's not enough. All these perils you mention are but the spice that will make his great outing memorable."

Fargo appealed to the count. "There's a difference between hunting bear and being hunted by Comanches. Talk it over with her. Make her see how loco this is."

"I'm sorry, Monsieur Fargo," Louis Tristan said, "but I very much agree with her."

"Oh, hell," Fargo said.

"You see, we have already been to Africa. That was just last year. We went because it, too, has a reputation for danger. So when Henriette proposed coming here, I liked the idea. But I'm not, as you might say, a dolt. I have it all planned out. In addition to ourselves, I've brought servants and nine men who are in my employ, with firearms for all. I will also hire locals for things like driving some of our wagons. Surely that is enough guns to discourage these Comanches of yours?"

Fargo sighed. "You're not listening."

Claude said, "No, American. It is you who doesn't use his ears. My brother-in-law has his heart set on this adventure, and with you or without you, we, his loved ones, have pledged to make his dream come true."

"You're all dumb as stumps," Fargo said.

Both Claude and the oldest son, Charles, looked ready to tear into him.

The youngest son, Philip, said, "To you we must appear to be so, *oui*. I have read enough stories to appreciate your position. I hope you can appreciate ours. This means the world to our *père*, to our father, and as our uncle has made clear, we want to do all we can to help him."

Fargo gazed around the table. Nothing he'd told them had sunk in. They had no inkling of what they were letting themselves in for.

"Would you like the night to think it over?" Louis asked.

"Would you and the men be willing to go and leave the ladies here?" Fargo asked.

"Why would you even suggest such a thing?" Claude demanded.

"He is being gallant," Henriette said. "He thinks to spare us females from harm." She shook her head. "I will speak for my daughters and my sister when I say that where the men go, we go."

"Even if it kills you?" Fargo said.

Henriette grinned. "Your flair for melodramatics amuses me. Many settlers live in west Texas, do they not? Families with women and children?"

"There are a few," Fargo admitted.

"You quibble, monsieur. There are more than a few, I have heard. And they go about their daily lives with little fear of the dangers you harp on."

"It's not the same," Fargo said. "They're used to it. They take precautions."

"As will we," Henriette said. She looked at the count. "I leave it for you to have the final word, my husband."

Louis placed his hand on her wrist and gently squeezed. *"Merci, mon cher."* He gazed down the table at Fargo. "As should be obvious, my family backs me in this. They think it will be good for me, and I think it will be good for me. I have weighed the perils and taken steps, not the least of which is to hire the best scout alive. That is, should you agree to guide us."

"And if you do not," Henriette said, "I am sure we can find someone else."

The twins broke their long silence. Blanche—or was it

Jeanne?—smiled and said, "Please do guide us, monsieur. My sister and I would be delighted."

"Indeed," the other vision agreed. "We would feel safe in your hands." As she said the word *hands*, her lips curled suggestively.

Fargo recognized a lost cause when he saw one. They'd go with or without him. And since they were so determined to ignore his warnings and get themselves killed, he might as well make the best of their stupidity. "I'll take the five thousand in advance."

Louis brightened and stood. "Does this mean you accept?" He clapped his hands. "*Merveilleuse.* We will go to a bank and I will deposit the money in your name, to be paid upon our return."

"On *my* return," Fargo said.

"Monsieur?" The count chuckled. "*Oui.* I see. In case your dire predictions come true. Very well. To be paid on your return to Corpus Christi."

"One moment, if you please," Claude said. "How do we know he won't desert us in the wilds and come back to claim his money prematurely?"

Fargo was on his feet before Claude stopped speaking. He came around the table and when Claude turned in his chair toward him, he punched him, a short, hard blow that rocked Claude's chair and caused it to teeter on its rear legs. Claude squawked and tried to grab the table, but he was too slow. The chair, and Claude, crashed to the floor.

Everyone else sat rooted in astonishment.

Swearing luridly in French, Claude shook his head to clear it and went to push erect.

A single stride and Fargo stood over him. Seizing Claude by the shirt, Fargo yanked him upright, and shoved.

Unable to keep his balance, Claude slammed against the wall.

"How dare you!" he raged, and launched into rapid-fire French.

"In this country," Fargo said, "when you call a man a cheat and a liar, you better be ready to back what you say."

"I will have your life for this, you despicable pig."

Smiling grimly, Fargo lowered his right hand so it brushed his holster. "You're welcome to try."

Claude glanced at Fargo's Colt, and swallowed. Opening his jacket, he said, "Surely you wouldn't shoot an unarmed man?"

"Not usually," Fargo said. "But in your case I might make an exception."

"Monsieur Fargo!" the count exclaimed, rising and hurrying around the table past his daughters. "Contain yourself."

Fargo stepped up to Claude, who shrank against the wall. "I don't like you, mister. Not even a little bit. Get on my bad side again and you'll spit out teeth."

"A childish threat," Claude blustered. "I would expect no less from your ilk."

"Ilk?" Fargo said, and cocked his fist to slug him in the gut.

"Please, monsieur," Louis said, and put himself between them. "There has been enough violence."

"This?" Fargo said, with a nod at Claude. "This is nothing compared to what you might run into out there." He motioned to the west.

Henriette was also on her feet. "Is this the sort of behavior we must put up with out on the prairie?"

"No," Fargo said, returning to his chair. "Out on the prairie I'd shoot him."

The count quickly said, "He jests, dear. A little joke at our expense."

"I'm not so sure," Henriette said.

Claude was smoothing his jacket and tugging on the ends of his sleeves. "I will not stand here and be mocked by a simple-minded frontiersman." He sniffed and moved to the door. "If anyone wants me I'll be in my cabin."

The door slammed after him.

"I hope you're happy," Henriette said. "Your crude antics have driven him off."

"Good riddance," Fargo said.

"Please, monsieur," Louis said. "As we will be together for a number of weeks, it behooves us to get along."

"Tell that to Claude." Fargo went to the door. "I'll be back in an hour."

"Wait," Louis said. "Where are you going? Does this mean you want to rethink my offer?"

"All it means," Fargo said, "is that I need a drink."

4

The Zachary was busy.

Fargo went to the far end of the bar. He ordered a whiskey and swallowed it in two gulps and beckoned for another.

"Are you sure you don't want a whole bottle?" the barman asked.

Fargo walked to a corner table and sat and pondered. He supposed he should go out and beat his head against a tree. It was loco to take that bunch off into the wilds. They weren't just asking for trouble; they were begging for it. They had no damn idea what they were in for.

Fargo sighed and sipped. He supposed if it wasn't for all the jackasses in the world, no one else could claim to have half a brain.

It didn't help that he was commencing to get a bad feeling in his gut. He didn't get that often, but when he did it was usually right, and his gut was telling him this would turn out badly.

He was about done when out of the back hall came a dove he'd noticed on his last visit. She had to be about thirty, but she'd preserved herself well and had long brown hair and a full body with watermelons for breasts, and wide hips. She smiled tiredly at him as she went by.

Fargo watched her order a drink and cradle it in both hands. Turning, she came toward the hall. He slid an empty chair out with his boot and said, "You're welcome to join me if you don't mind the company."

She stopped and regarded him with more than mild interest. "A little early, ain't it, for what you might have in mind?"

"How early does it have to be to get drunk and get laid?" Fargo asked, and grinned.

"Oh-ho," she said, and eased into the chair. "The name is Cecelia, but everyone calls me Big Tits."

"A man would need a ladder to climb them," Fargo joked.

Cecelia snorted and laughed. "They started sprouting when I was ten. You should have seen the boys. Drew them like honey draws bears."

"I like honey," Fargo said.

Cecelia tilted her head. "I bet you do. You look like honey your own self."

Fargo drank. Now that he'd drawn her to his table, he didn't have a whole lot to say.

Fortunately, Cecelia had no such problem. "Usually I sleep until two or three in the afternoon, but I was tossing and turning back there." She nodded at the hall. "I have a room. It's cheaper than staying at a boardinghouse. One day I'll have saved enough and then it's so long to Corpus Christi and so long to Texas."

"You sound like a gal with a plan."

"Damn right," Cecelia declared. "I'm going to Denver. I hear a woman can make a good living there. They say it has a lot of classy houses."

"That it does," Fargo confirmed.

"You've been there?"

Fargo nodded.

All interest, Cecelia leaned on her elbows. "So, do you think I'm right to go?"

"If it's money you're after, Denver is as good as anywhere."

Cecelia looked down at herself. "At my age money is important. My looks won't last a whole lot longer. Five years, maybe ten if I'm real careful. I need to squirrel some away for my rocking-chair years."

"Or find a horny gent with deep pockets."

Cecelia chuckled. "There's that. So far, though, I haven't found one who'd like to ride me full-time." She looked him up and down. "How about you?"

"I am a onetime only," Fargo said, "and my pockets are shallow."

"Too bad," Cecelia said. "You're awful easy on the eyes."

"So, is it too early for you?" Fargo thought to clarify.

"Honey, any hour of the day or night, my pump is primed."

Cecelia grinned and winked. "I've never said no in my life. Which, come to think of it, is probably how I wound up here."

"Want another drink?" Fargo offered.

"No, thanks. One is my limit before sunset. I need it to get the blood flowing. Know what I mean?"

"Do I ever?" Fargo said.

"So, what do you do, handsome? We don't see a lot of buckskins in these parts. Corpus Christi has become civilized."

"I scout, mostly," Fargo said.

"For the army and the like?" Cecelia made clucking sounds. "I could never do what you do. Too risky. Just last night a man was telling me that the Comanches are acting up again."

"What man?" This was news to Fargo. The last he'd heard, things had been quiet.

"I didn't ask his name. He came in from San Antonio way or some such. He said that the Comanches have raided a bunch of farms."

"Wonderful," Fargo said.

"Are you all right? You look as if you just swallowed a handful of sour grapes."

"Life is never easy," Fargo said.

Cecelia nodded. "I hear that. It sure as hell hasn't been easy for me. I'm not complaining, mind you. Only saying how it is." She emptied her glass and let out a contented "Ahhh. That hit the spot. How about you? Care to give me a whirl?"

"Don't mind if I do." Fargo sucked down the last of his bug juice, smacked the glass on the table, and followed her down the hall to a door on the right. She opened it and motioned for him to go in first.

The room was small but nicely furnished with a bed and a table and a gilded mirror. There was a washbasin and a small woodstove and a worn rug fraying along the edges.

"It ain't much but it's comfortable," Cecelia said. She closed the door and leaned back with her hands behind her and a seductive smile on her ruby lips. "See anything you like?" She gave a saucy swirl to her hips.

Stepping over, Fargo cupped her breast with his right hand and cupped her lower down with his left.

Cecelia stiffened and gasped and her smile widened. "Oh my. You get right to it, don't you?"

Fargo shut her up by covering her mouth with his. Her soft lips parted and her wet tongue darted out. He sucked on it as if it were hard honey, and she returned the favor by sucking on his.

"Mmmmm," Cecelia cooed when they parted. "You sure kiss awful nice."

Fargo hiked her dress and the light cotton chemise she wore underneath and caressed her inner thighs. She shuddered slightly, and her breath became hotter. When he delved between her legs, she gasped and hungrily molded her mouth to his. His right hand, meanwhile, had undone enough buttons to slide in and under and cup her breast anew. Her nipple was as rigid as a tack. When he pinched it she rose onto the tips of her toes and nipped at his neck with her teeth.

Her own neck smelled of lilac water, and her hair had a minty scent.

Fargo nearly gasped when her fingers found his member. His pants were about to burst, he was so hard. She stroked and rubbed and for a second he thought he might explode. Only through force of will did he contain himself.

"My, oh my," Cecelia breathed. "You should start your own stud farm."

Chuckling, Fargo steered her toward the bed. Bodies glued, she fell onto her back and he went with her.

Lying on his side, he kissed and licked her neck and her ear. She wriggled and exhaled and dug her nails into his shoulder.

"I want you," Cecelia husked. "And I'm not just saying that because you're paying me."

Fargo licked across her throat to her other ear. She liked having her lobe tickled by the tip of his tongue. She also liked it when his forefinger slid along her moist slit to her tiny button.

"Oh!" Cecelia quietly cried. And again, "Oh yes."

Fargo went on kissing and licking and rimming until she was panting with desire. Her eyes were hooded; her hips moved in continuous gyration.

"Come on and do me, big man," Cecelia begged. "I wasn't kidding when I said I want it."

Ignoring her request, Fargo parted her dress so he could devote himself to her melons. They were pendulous yet firm. When he pulled on a nipple, stretching it near to ripping it off,

20

she tried to suck his mouth into hers and humped against him as if to buck him off the bed.

"More of that," Cecelia said. "Please."

Happy to oblige, Fargo filled his mouth with as much of a breast as he could and sucked and worked and bit ever so lightly. Cecelia squirmed. She uttered low cries. She spread her legs wide and wrapped them around his waist, locking her ankles behind him.

Fargo paused. He'd forgotten a few things. He undid his gun belt and dropped it to the floor. He took off his spurs and then his hat and added them to the pile. Last, he started to pull his pants down, but she slapped his hands away and tugged for him until his pants were down around his shins.

"I can't wait much longer," Cecelia complained.

Settling onto his knees, Fargo reached for his member, but she slapped his hand again and grasped it herself. A gleam came into her eyes and she ran her hand down and up several times. Again she almost made him explode. Then, grinning like a she-cat in heat, she fed him into her inch by slow inch.

A constriction formed in Fargo's throat. Her sheath clung to his pole as if made to fit. He moved just a little and she gripped his shoulders and shook. It took a few seconds for him to realize, with some surprise, that she was gushing. Usually it took longer.

At length Cecelia subsided and looked up at him. "There's something about you."

"About me how?" Fargo asked.

"I don't rightly know. I haven't figured it out yet. But you get to me."

"Do I, now?" Fargo said, and thrust up into her as if to impale her. Her eyes grew huge and her mouth formed an O and she met each rapier drive of his cock with her velvet pussy. He went faster, and harder. She did the same.

It was a while before he reached the crest. He sailed over the abyss on a floodtide of pleasure and then slowly sank onto his side next to Cecelia, oblivious of the world.

After he knew not how long, he roused and drowsily opened his eyes.

A man was standing across the room, pointing a revolver at him.

5

The first thing Fargo noticed, strangely enough, was the man's revolver. It wasn't like any he knew. At one time or another he'd seen every model that Colt, Smith & Wesson, and Remington manufactured, as well as many six-shooters produced by smaller firms. Never, ever, had he set eyes on a revolver like this. The frame was thin, the barrel little more than a pencil, and the butt appeared to be half the size of his Colt's.

Then Fargo looked at the man. The intruder wore seaman's garb, complete with a kind of cap that only those who plied the waves favored. But they didn't suit him. Or, rather, they didn't quite fit him. The shirt was too big; the pants were too loose. It was plain the clothes weren't his. The man had apparently donned them as some sort of disguise.

Fargo glanced at the floor, and his Colt.

The man took a step and wagged his unusual revolver. At the same time he put a finger to his lips and nodded at Cecelia.

Just then she let out a light snore.

The man motioned for Fargo to stand. Quietly, Fargo did so, pulling up his pants as he straightened. Buckling the belt, he raised his arms. The man backed to the door, which was partway open. He opened it wider, ducked his head out and looked both ways, and motioned for Fargo to follow him.

Resisting an impulse to dive for his Colt, Fargo complied. He reasoned that if the man wanted to kill him, he'd already be dead. For the life of him, though, he couldn't figure what the man wanted.

His abductor kept the revolver trained on his chest as they turned and went the short way to the back door. It was partway open, too. The man pushed it with his foot and eased out, indicating that Fargo should do the same.

"Who are you?" Fargo asked.

The man didn't answer.

"What the hell is this about?"

Once again, the man didn't respond.

They were in a small fenced yard. The fence was about six feet high. A gate led out into an alley. To one side was a woodshed. To the other an empty stall for a horse.

"What do you want, damn it?"

The man was scanning the nearby buildings. Or so Fargo thought until he realized that the man was looking at the windows. Probably to make sure no one was looking out.

The man cocked his revolver and there was a tiny *click*. He extended his arm to shoot.

Behind Fargo, there was the sound of someone yawning and Cecelia came shuffling out, her dress in disarray, her hair disheveled. She was scratching her head and squinting against the glare of the sun. "What's going on, handsome?" she said. "I caught a glimpse of you—"

The intruder pointed his gun at her.

Fargo sprang. He was on his would-be assassin in a bound. The man tried to train the revolver on him, but Fargo slammed his fist against the man's forearm and the revolver went flying. Instantly the man retreated and his other hand swept from behind his back holding a double-edged dagger. He stabbed at Fargo's chest. That Fargo evaded it was luck more than anything; he started to skip out of reach and tripped over his own foot. The dagger flashed past, missing him by inches.

Before Fargo could regain his balance, the man was on him. The glittering blade flashed at Fargo's throat. Fargo sidestepped, swiveled, and landed a solid punch that sent his assailant stumbling. The man recovered and came at him again, slashing and stabbing.

Retreating, Fargo somehow ended up near the woodshed.

Darting aside, he grabbed a log about two feet long and as thick as his arm. It made a dandy club. When the seeming seaman launched himself, the dagger poised, Fargo swung. He connected, too, with a loud *thud* and the distinct crack of what might be a rib.

Crying out, the man dropped to his hands and knees.

He clutched himself and scrambled back and cursed viciously— in French.

"What the hell?" Fargo said. He raised the club to swing it again.

Recoiling, the man spotted the fallen revolver and scrabbled toward it.

"Look out!" Cecelia hollered.

Fargo darted in and brought the log down, but the man rolled out of harm's way. He went to swing again.

The killer pushed to his feet and whirled. His hands outstretched, he leaped and caught hold of the top of the fence and swung up and over.

"He's getting away," Cecelia cried.

Fargo reached the fence, threw the club down, and gripped the top. He began to pull himself up. Gleaming steel streaked at his face and he let go and backpedaled.

"What are you doing?" Cecelia asked.

"Shut the hell up."

Fargo darted to a different spot and peered over. The assassin was flying down the alley with the speed of a natural-born sprinter.

It only took a moment for Fargo to climb over and give chase. He was swift of foot, but when he came to the thoroughfare at the alley's end and looked both ways, the man was nowhere to be seen.

"Damn."

Fargo ran a short distance one way, and then turned and ran the other. He attracted attention but he didn't care. After going half a block, he drew up.

The assassin had gotten away.

Fargo turned back. That the man was French could only mean one thing: He was part of the count's party, and had been set on him by one of the count's family. Why any of them would want him dead was beyond him. Unless—and Fargo scowled at the idea—the man was sent by Claude Dupree to pay him back for hitting him.

Another possibility occurred to him. Could it be, Fargo asked himself, that someone didn't want him to be the count's guide? He couldn't imagine why.

Cecelia was waiting at the gate. "What on earth was that about? Who was that jasper?"

"I don't know," Fargo said, "and I don't care."

"He got away? Could be he'll try again." She touched his cheek. "You'd best have eyes in the back of your head."

They returned to her room. Fargo strapped on his gun belt and offered her ten dollars.

"You don't really need to," Cecelia said.

"Yes," Fargo said, "I do." He pushed the coins into her hand, kissed her, and left. If he'd had any lingering doubts about accepting the count's offer, the attempt on his life had erased them. Whoever sicced the fake seaman on him had made the biggest mistake of their life. He wouldn't rest until he settled the score.

A carriage was parked below the gangway to the *Relaise*. Fargo had never seen one so fancy. The driver wore a uniform with large silver buttons and a high hat with a silver brim. The man nodded at him as he turned to go up the gangway.

Voices sounded, speaking French, and none other than Count Louis Tristan appeared. He, too, wore a high hat, and a cape, of all things. He was holding a gold-handled cane.

Henriette was with him. She had changed into a blue dress with dark blue trim and was carrying a matching parasol.

Behind them came the twins, Blanche and Jeanne. When they saw Fargo, both smiled and waved.

Fargo scanned the deck. A few hands were busy swabbing, and at other tasks. He had a hunch that if he searched the vessel from end to end, he just might find the assassin.

"Monsieur Fargo!" the count happily declared. "You are punctual. I like that."

"When someone is giving me five thousand dollars," Fargo said, "I'm punctual as hell."

"Your language, monsieur, if you please," Henriette said, with a tilt of her head at the twins. "There are ladies present."

The girls giggled.

"Honestly, Henriette," Louis said.

"Is it too much to ask that our scout conduct himself like a gentleman?" Henriette rejoined.

"Why don't you ask your scout?" Fargo said.

Henriette regarded him haughtily. "Very well. I respectfully request that you refrain from using vulgar language around my family. I realize that you are probably accustomed to the habit. But will you at least try?"

"I sure as hell will," Fargo said.

More giggling from the twins.

The driver climbed down. He lowered the step and opened the door and stood aside and bowed.

Fargo nodded at the carriage. "Don't tell me," he said. "You brought your own instead of renting one?"

"But of course," Louis said.

"It must be nice to be rich."

"It is," Louis said. He held Henriette's hand as she climbed in and did the same for each of his daughters. "After you, monsieur," he said.

Fargo had been in carriages before but never one like this. It was all leather and polished wood, with silver trim, and smelled as fresh as the day it was made. He sat on the front seat next to the twins, facing Henriette.

Louis clambered up and settled himself next to his wife. He smoothed his cape and flicked a piece of lint.

"I can't tell you how happy you have made me by agreeing to guide us."

"Let's see if you're still as happy when it's over," Fargo said.

Henriette said, "Are you always such a pessimist, monsieur scout?"

"I see things as they are," Fargo told her, "not as I might like them to be."

"You're suggesting we are blind to the perils we might encounter?"

"I'm saying you don't know what you're in for," Fargo said.

Louis coughed. "Let's not start that again, shall we? If we've misjudged, so be it. But I have every confidence that I've taken every precaution that can be made."

Above them the driver's whip cracked and the carriage lurched into motion.

Fargo noticed that Blanche—or was it Jeanne?—was sitting so close to him, their legs brushed. He glanced at her from under his hat brim and saw that she was looking at him out of the corner of her eye. He grinned and winked.

The girl glanced at her parents, who were gazing out the windows, and then back at him. Shifting her shoulders so her bosom swelled against her dress, she ran the pink tip of her tongue along her full lips, grinned, and returned his wink.

The other twin giggled.

"I think you will find, Monsieur Fargo," the count was saying, "that this will be a most enjoyable experience for you."

"It might have its moments," Fargo said.

6

It was quite a caravan, as the count called it.

Besides Fargo and the Frenchman and his family, there were fourteen servants. Fargo had asked why there were so many and Louis said that only four were his. The rest tended to the needs of his wife and children, and Claude and Odette had three of their own. In addition, there were the workers the count had brought with him from France, and Texans hired to drive wagons and the like.

Now, drawing rein, Fargo shifted in the saddle and looked back. The winding column stretched almost a quarter of a mile long.

The count rode a grand white horse that moved with a high-stepping gait as if it were on parade. He smiled as Fargo swung alongside. "At last, to have my dream come true. Here we are, in the wilds. I can't tell you how invigorated I am."

Fargo didn't point out that they were barely five miles out of Corpus Christi and nowhere near the "wilds."

"We need to keep everyone closer together," he advised.

"I beg your pardon?"

Fargo indicated the line extending to the southeast. "We're too stretched out. Have your people bunch up more."

"Ah," Louis said, and nodded. "Very well. See to it."

"Me?"

"You are our scout, are you not? I leave all matters having to do with how we travel in your capable hands."

"How many of your people speak English?" Fargo asked.

"My family does. It is a second language in my country. A few of our servants have a smattering. And perhaps half a dozen of—" Louis stopped. "I see your point. How can you give them orders when they can't understand you? Very well." He twisted and crooked an arm at his sons. "Philip! Come here on the double. I must have words with you."

The youngest son, Fargo noticed, rode fairly well.

For that matter, all of them did. He mentioned it as Philip approached.

"*Merci* for the compliment," Louis said. "I have a stable on my estate at Marseilles, and I have made all my children ride from an early age. Henriette is quite the breeder. And her sister and Claude both have experience with horses."

That was something at least, Fargo reflected. He gazed back down the column. Henriette, Odette, and Claude were together off to one side, as they'd been since leaving Corpus Christi.

Philip came up. "*Oui, mon père?*"

"I have a task for you, son," Louis said. "I know how much you have looked forward to this. You read all you could find on the American frontier."

"I am more excited than I have ever been," Philip declared. He breathed deep of the muggy air. "To think, we are actually here."

"How would you like to be second-in-command under Monsieur Fargo?"

"Papa?"

"You heard me. Monsieur Fargo needs someone to be his liaison with the men. You can be second under him, our second scout, as it were."

"But, Papa," Philip said, "I know nothing about scouting. Only what I have read."

"Monsieur Fargo will teach you what you need to know. Is that not right, Monsieur?"

Fargo almost said no. He had no hankering to take a green pup under his wing.

Then Philip turned admiring eyes on him and said, "Would you, monsieur? I would be ever so grateful. To learn from a great frontiersman such as yourself. Someone who knows this land so well. Who has fought the red man and hunted buffalo. Who has—"

"Hell," Fargo said. "I'll do it on one condition."

"Monsieur?" Philip said.

"You're to do exactly as I say when I say to do it. No questions asked."

29

"But, monsieur, how will I learn if I don't ask?"

The count interjected, "He means in emergencies, I am sure." Leaning over, he clapped his youngest on the arm. "Congratulations. You are now an assistant scout."

"I am in heaven," Philip exclaimed.

Fargo gave his first order. "Go back down the line. Tell everyone that they are to be no more than twenty feet behind whoever is in front of them. Wagons or riders, it makes no difference. No straggling. Savvy?"

"Oh, *oui*, monsieur, I savvy completely and fully," Philip said. "It is so we can close ranks quickly if we are attacked, is that not so? I read about how wagon trains circle when they are set upon by savages. In *The Many Perils of Prairie Annie*, there was this part where—"

Fargo held up a hand. "Go."

"Oh. *Oui*. Sorry." Philip beamed and reined around and slapped his short legs.

"Kids," Fargo said.

Louis chuckled. "Be patient with him, I beg you. He is a good son."

Hooves drummed, and Charles joined them. He cast a glance of disapproval at Fargo and said to his father, "What is going on with Philip? He rode past me grinning like a demented ape."

The count explained, adding, "Please don't be offended that I chose him and not you. As the older, you naturally should have been my first choice."

"Oh, please," Charles said. "Am I five years old, to be jealous of my sibling? And besides"—he stared out across the rolling grassland and his mouth curled in distaste—"I have no interest in this country or its crude inhabitants. I'm only here because of Mother and her insane idea."

"Have a care, Charles," Louis said. "Show more respect."

"Father, I have the highest respect for both of you. You know that," Charles said. "But this—" He gestured with contempt. "It can only end badly."

"I will thank you not to voice your opinion to the others," Louis said. "I won't have you spoil our expedition with your pessimism." He jabbed his heels and reined around toward his wife.

Charles saw Fargo staring at him and said, "What?"

"You don't like me and I sure as hell don't like you," Fargo said, "but we agree this won't end well."

"It is lunacy," Charles said.

Fargo nodded. "I'll do my best to keep your family alive, but there's only so much I can do."

"You might not believe this, but I appreciate your sentiment," Charles said, and sighed. "I tried to talk them out of it. I practically begged my mother not to present her idea to my father and then practically begged him not to come. But do you think either would listen?"

"You care for them that much?" Fargo said.

"They are my father and mother," Charles said a trifle indignantly. "But no, it was not entirely that. It's this country of yours."

"How's that again?"

"You Americans," Charles said. "You are pathetic barbarians pretending to be civilized. And I am not talking about the primitive red man. I am talking about you and your ilk."

"You like that word," Fargo said, remembering that Charles had used it on the ship.

"Monsieur, it is an undisputable fact that your backwater country is hundreds of years behind the more advanced nations—"

"Like France?" Fargo interrupted.

"Exactly. Our culture is a beacon to the world. Surely you have heard of the Renaissance? The great Enlightenment? And that is but one of our many accomplishments. Culture flourishes in my country.

"But here"—Charles stopped and scowled—"here you have men such as yourself, who wear animal skins and know nothing of things that matter. Literature. Poetry. The arts. Fine cuisine. The theater. I could go on but why bother?"

"Well, aren't you full of yourself?" Fargo said.

"I take pride in my country, monsieur," Charles said. "Can you say the same?"

"This isn't about countries. It's about them." And Fargo bobbed his head at Louis and the others.

"In that we are in accord," Charles said. "So, though I despise you and all you represent, I will do whatever is necessary to keep them alive." He dipped at the waist as if bowing, and wheeled his mount.

"This gets better and better," Fargo said to the ovaro. He decided to ride on ahead and raised his reins, only to have two riders come up on either side of the stallion. Perfume tingled his nose. "Ladies," he said, and smiled.

The twins wore matching outfits and hats that made them impossible to tell apart. Both were grinning and both had twinkles in their eyes.

"Philip just told us that we are to stay close to each other," said the one on the right.

"And we thought we would stay close to you," said the one on the left.

They both giggled.

"What would your mother say?" Fargo said.

"We are almost of age, monsieur," said the twin on the right.

"We do as we please," said the other. "Discreetly, of course."

"*Oui,*" said the first twin. "We are models of discretion."

"Especially at night," said the second.

Fargo studied first the one and then the other. "How do I tell you two apart?"

The beauty on the right tittered. "I will tell you a secret, monsieur. We are not exactly alike."

"*Non,*" said the lovely on the left. "One of us has a birthmark on her thigh, and the other has a birthmark on her breast."

Fargo imagined them naked, and his mouth went dry with a hunger that had nothing to do with food. "Doesn't help me much unless you take off those dresses."

"Not in broad daylight, monsieur," said the twin on the right.

"How about this?" the other said, and reaching up, she pulled a pearl-tipped pin from the side of her hat and stuck it in the front. "Now you can tell us apart. I will wear my pin this way and Jeanne will wear hers on the side."

"So you're Blanche."

"*Peut-être,*" the girl said with another giggle. "Perhaps. Or perhaps we are teasing."

"We tease a lot," said the one who might be Jeanne. "We trust you do not mind?"

Fargo thought of the long nights ahead. "So long as I get to see those birthmarks, you can tease the hell out of me."

7

The burning summer heat had turned the prairie dry and brown, which was why Fargo stuck close to the Nueces River. That many people, that many animals, needed a lot of water. And, too, the woodland that bordered the river was rich with game. In the river itself were bass and other fish, and turtles and frogs.

At the outset Fargo stayed close to the count and the column. It would be a few days before he started to worry about Comanches and other hostiles; they usually roamed farther north.

The first night was a revelation. Henriette took charge of the personal staff, and Fargo had to hand it to her. The tents were up in no time. Cook fires were kindled, and the cook—they brought their very own chef—soon had tantalizing aromas wafting on the air.

The women helped Henriette while the men sat around a fire drinking and relaxing. Louis, Philip, and Charles passed a silver flask back and forth. Claude Dupree sipped from a crystal glass.

Fargo saw to the picketing of the horses and the placement of the wagons before he ventured to join them. Squatting, he accepted the flask from Philip, chugged, and grimaced. "What in God's name is this?"

"Crème de Noyaux," Philip said. "A favorite of my father's."

"It is most delicious," Louis said.

Fargo passed the flask back. "It tastes like hell." The flavor reminded him of hickory, or some kind of nut. "Don't you have whiskey?"

"I'm afraid not, monsieur," Louis said.

Charles sipped from his glass and said, "Do you see, American? Even your liquor shows your country's lack of culture and class."

"Charles," Louis said.

Philip said, "Please. Can we not have the usual petty squabbling? We should all be happy. So far, everything has gone nicely."

"So far," Fargo said.

"It is something, nonetheless," Philip said. He gave a start as a yip sounded out of the darkling plain. "My word. What was that?"

"We call them coyotes," Fargo said.

"I thought it might be a wolf," Philip said. "I'm told they are common here."

"Used to be," Fargo said. "Most of the wolves east of the Mississippi River have been killed off for the bounties on their pelts. Those out here tend to fight shy of people."

"Do these coyotes pose a threat to our horses?" Charles asked.

"I've never heard tell of a coyote attacking a horse," Fargo said. "It's the rattlers and prairie dog holes you have to watch out for."

"By rattlers you mean rattlesnakes?" Philip said.

"No, he means buffalo," Charles said sarcastically.

Ignoring him, Philip said, "But why prairie dog holes?"

"Your horse steps in one, it could break a leg."

Just then a servant came up, gave a bow, and said something in French.

"He informs us that dinner is served," Louis translated. "Monsieur Fargo, I would be pleased if you would join us in our tent."

"We're not eating out here?" Fargo said.

"Perish forbid," Louis declared. "My wife would not hear of it. We must observe the amenities, even in the wilderness."

Fargo had only ever seen one tent bigger than the count's and that was with a traveling circus. From a high pole flew a banner emblazoned with the Tristan crest: a knight in armor slaying a wild boar.

Earlier Fargo had witnessed several of the men take the parts of a table from a wagon and put it together. Now there it sat, covered with a white cloth, the silverware laid out with folded napkins, and a large candlestick holder in the center.

Chairs had been arranged, and the women were standing behind theirs, waiting for the men to seat them.

Louis went to Henriette's and held it out for her. Claude did likewise for Odette. Philip and Charles held out chairs for their sisters.

Fargo pulled out his own and sat. Instantly, a servant was at his side, filling his glass with water from a pitcher.

"This is the life, is it not?" the count said as he took his own seat at the head of the table. "All the comforts, yet we are in the wilds."

"You brought your own furniture," Fargo said.

"Including our beds," one of the twins said, and giggled. Neither was wearing a hat, so he couldn't tell who was who.

"Blanche," Henriette said, "we do not indulge in risqué talk at the table."

"Or anywhere else," Louis said.

"It has always amused me," Claude said, "that we are so delicate about discussing romance when we have a reputation for being the greatest lovers in the world."

Fargo snorted.

"I beg your pardon, monsieur?" Claude said. "Are you suggesting we're not?"

"I made love to a French woman once," Fargo said. "A fallen dove down to New Orleans, just in from Paris. She was fun but I wouldn't call her great."

"Monsieur Fargo!" Henriette exclaimed. "How could you, in front of my daughters?"

Blanche and Jeanne were glittering with interest. "Do you remember her name, monsieur?" the former asked.

Henriette smacked the table. "That will be quite enough. We don't care what her name was. Or why she stooped to such a level."

"She needed to eat," Fargo said.

"Excuse me?"

"She lost her husband and had three mouths to feed and had no other way of making money."

"Nonsense," Claude said. "She could have worked as a cook or a seamstress or indentured herself. Our servants earn enough to provide for their families."

"She had too much pride for that."

"Are you suggesting, monsieur, that being a servant was beneath her?"

"Some folks don't like licking other folks' boots," Fargo said.

Henriette sniffed. "That is not what our servants do at all. We treat them with the utmost respect."

"But they're still servants," Fargo said.

"I miss your point."

The count coughed. "I flatter myself that I take it, my dear. Monsieur Fargo is American, and Americans place a great premium on their freedom. To him, being a servant is the same as being a slave. Am I right, monsieur?"

"I wouldn't go that far."

"But you would never, as you so quaintly put it"—and the count smiled—"lick another person's boots."

"Not while I'm breathing."

The talk turned to the long day in the saddle.

Charles complained that he was stiff. Odette said that she might ride on one of the wagons tomorrow. The count mentioned how there had been too little game, and Fargo let him know that the farther they went from civilization, the more wildlife they'd run into.

"*Excellente,*" Louis said. "I did not bring my hunting rifles all this way not to use them. I hope to shoot a buffalo and have the head stuffed and mounted in my study. My friends will be envious."

"We might run into a few buffs before too long," Fargo said.

"I sincerely hope so."

At that juncture supper was served.

Fargo had been to his share of fancy restaurants. And on more than several occasions he'd eaten with those who were well-to-do. But never, ever, had he seen a meal like this.

It started with soup. Fargo wasn't much of a soup eater, but he gave it a try. After three spoonfuls he set down his spoon. It was brown water, nothing more. There were no vegetables, no chunks of meat.

Next, amazingly, came a bowl of oysters. Fargo wasn't a big oyster eater, either, but at least it was something he could chew.

After that there were strips of fish and grouse, both bought in Corpus Christi and brought along for the occasion.

Fargo would eat fish when he had to, but give him a delicious piece of grouse any day. He ate half a bird, thinking it was the main course. He was mistaken.

Vegetables were served, and a salad for those who wanted one. A platter was set down heaped with slabs of roast beef.

Fargo wished he hadn't eaten so much grouse; he liked beef even more. He dug in, anyway, and was lavish with the salt.

"You know," Charles said at one point, "this American beef isn't half bad."

"*Oui*," Henriette said. "But the cook had to go to a lot of trouble to trim off all the fat."

Fargo stared at the piece on his plate. "Why in hell did he do that?"

"I beg your pardon?" Henriette said.

"You had him cut out the best part of the meat."

Henriette's nose crinkled. "Don't tell me Americans *eat* fat? Haven't you heard that it's bad for the digestion?"

"Lady," Fargo said bluntly, "I'd rather have a juicy piece of fat in my mouth than just about anything." He almost added, "Except tit."

"How disgusting."

"Now, now, my dear," Louis said. "Different countries have different customs. I have heard that in Turkey they eat only sheep, and in Japan they are fond of a soup made from snake urine."

The twins giggled.

"Enough, if you please," Henriette said. "I will not have my meal ruined by the disgusting habits of other cultures."

After the main course, or the *plat* as the count referred to it, came several jellies and something called a soufflé. His hosts ate their soufflés with relish, but Fargo didn't see what the fuss was about. It tasted of lemon, and made him pucker.

They washed down their food with coffee.

Fargo had four cups. He was idly listening to their chatter and almost missed it when the count said his name. "What was that?"

"I was wondering if we should post guards tonight. We're not into Indian country yet, so is there really a need?"

"We post guards every night." Fargo set him straight. "No matter where we are."

Presently the meal ended. Fargo thanked them and rose to go check on the ovaro. It was picketed with the other horses. He passed a crackling fire ringed by half a dozen of the men, and one of them happened to look up.

Fargo stopped short.

It was the would-be assassin from Corpus Christi.

8

The man was wearing a hat with a wide brim and a baggy shirt and pants. Their eyes met, and for an instant the assassin froze. Then he leaped to his feet and bolted.

Fargo went after him. There were surprised shouts from some of the others as he raced around the fire and into the darkness.

Damn, the man could run. Fargo saw him glance back and go even faster.

The camp was behind them, the woods that bordered the river ahead.

Fargo pumped his legs. He refused to let the killer get away a second time. He drew his Colt but didn't shoot. To hit someone on the fly at night was pure chance, and he wanted to be sure. He frowned when the assassin reached the trees and was swallowed by the vegetation. Not slowing, he came to the same spot and plunged in after him.

He went a dozen feet and stopped. He was being reckless. The noise he was making, the man could shoot at the sound.

Fargo scoured the benighted forest. Nothing moved.

In the distance an owl hooted and far to the north a wolf howled. He warily skirted an oak and some briars and smothered a burst of frustration. He had lost the bastard a second time.

Fargo straightened. He started to turn and a forearm clamped across his windpipe from behind even as an iron hand seized the wrist to his gun hand and he was wrenched violently backward and slammed against a tree.

"I have you, American!" the man hissed in his ear.

Fargo's body was a mass of pain; his throat was on fire. He tried to bring the Colt to bear but couldn't raise his arm. He sought to suck in air, without success. Desperate for breath, he dug his heels into the soil and levered backward, seeking to unbalance the assassin and break free. The man tottered, and they both went down.

The grip on his throat didn't let up, and if he didn't do something, and do it quickly, his throat would be crushed.

The only thing Fargo could think of was to ram his head back into the man's face. He was rewarded with a yelp. He rammed his right elbow into the man's ribs and then his left, and the hold on his throat slackened but not enough for him to breathe. His head was spinning and he was on the verge of passing out. Frantic, he drove his head back a second time and blood splattered his neck. He rolled, bearing the man with him, and got his free arm under him. With a powerful surge, he made it to his knees. Reaching over his shoulder, he clawed at the man's face. His nails dug into yielding flesh and grew wet with more blood. The man cursed in French and attempted to firm his hold.

Fargo shifted, twisted, slammed his elbow into the man's gut. And hurt him, too, because the man cried out and released him.

Sucking in deep breaths, Fargo heaved to his feet. His right arm was struck a jarring blow and his Colt went flying. Stooping, he clutched at his pant leg and in another moment the Arkansas toothpick was molded to his palm.

The assassin had a knife, too. Steel glittered in the starlight as the man crouched and moved it from side to side.

"Who are you?" Fargo rasped.

The man stopped wagging the knife.

"What's this about?"

"It is about you dying, American," the assassin growled, and was on him in a rush.

Fargo countered a stab. Blade rang on blade and the man circled anew. Crouching, Fargo feinted right and went left. He nicked the other's sleeve. The man tried a feint, but Fargo dodged.

Shouts came from the camp. Fargo was aware of lights, lanterns and torches, coming toward the river.

The assassin was aware of them, too. He glanced at them, and swore.

"Drop your knife and I'll let you live," Fargo offered. Dead, the man couldn't tell him anything.

"Go to hell."

Their weapons flashed.

Fargo blocked a stab intended for his arm. He slashed the man's side and the man retreated but only far enough to touch his ribs and stare at the blood on his fingers.

"Damn you," the assassin snarled. "Most would have been dead by now."

"Like them easy, do you?" Fargo taunted.

The yells and the lights were closer.

With a sideways bound, the man fled. The move caught Fargo off guard. He was a shade slow in pursuing and in only a dozen strides he lost sight of him. He turned every which way and didn't spot him.

It was Fargo's turn to swear.

"Monsieur Fargo? Monsieur Fargo?" Louis called out. "Where are you?"

Fargo didn't answer. Poised to spring, he was waiting for the assassin to move and give himself away.

"Monsieur Fargo?"

That sounded like Philip. There were women's voices, too. The whole family must be out looking.

It was with the utmost reluctance that Fargo moved into the open. "Here," he said as light spilled over him and shadowed shapes converged.

"Monsieur Fargo!" the count exclaimed.

"Are you all right?" Philip asked.

"We were told you chased a man from our camp," Henriette said. "Who was it, and why?"

The twins, for once, weren't grinning or giggling. Charles was somber. Claude had an arm around Odette's shoulders.

"Well?" Louis prompted. "Speak, man. We are anxious to hear."

"One of you is out to kill me," Fargo informed them.

"What are you talking about?" Henriette said. "Why would any of us want you dead?"

Fargo told them about the attempt on his life in Corpus Christi, and the chase into the woods.

"One of our own men?" Louis said in disbelief. "Impossible."

41

He turned to his sons. "Charles, Philip, have all of the help gather in front of our tent. I will question them personally and get to the bottom of this outrage."

The pair hurried off.

"If you ask me," Claude said, "Monsieur Fargo is mistaken. He only thought he saw the man who he says tried to kill him."

"Then why did the man run?" Louis said.

Claude shrugged. "Monsieur Fargo went at him and he was afraid for his life and fled."

"That is too thin, Claude," the count said. "No, I believe it happened exactly as Monsieur Fargo has told us it did."

To Fargo's considerable surprise, Henriette came over and put a hand on his arm.

"I am most sorry, monsieur, that you were set upon. It is this country of yours. It is too barbaric."

"Describe the man who was going to shoot you," Louis requested, "in as much detail as you can."

Fargo complied.

"I do not recall anyone answering that description," Louis said. "But then, I do not pay much attention to the workers." He turned to his wife. "How about you, my dear? I left the bringing of help and the hiring in your hands. Do we employ someone who fits?"

"I have not paid much attention to them, either," Henriette said. "And besides, I delegated the task to Claude."

Everyone looked at the brother-in-law.

"*Oui,*" Claude said. "I hired men to handle the wagons and other chores, as instructed. But I don't recall anyone answering that description."

Fargo headed for camp.

"Wait, monsieur," the count said. "Where are you going?"

"I need a drink." Fargo went straight to his saddle and bed-roll and opened his saddlebags. He'd intended to save the bottle he'd brought for later on. Opening it, he tilted it to his lips and chugged. The burning sensation that spread down his throat to his gut was like a tonic.

"Monsieur, I specifically forbid the bringing of liquor on our expedition," Louis said.

The count and his wife had followed him.

"Didn't you hear my husband?" Henriette demanded.

"I heard him." Fargo swallowed more Monongahela, and sighed. "Care for a swig, Louis?" He held out the bottle.

The count looked at it longingly but didn't take it.

"I will thank you to address my husband as Monsieur Tristan or Count Tristan," Henriette said. "That you are in our employ does not give you the right to be familiar."

"God, you're a pain in the ass," Fargo said.

Henriette turned so red, it was a wonder her head didn't explode. "How dare you talk to me that way? You will treat me with the respect I deserve."

"I am," Fargo said, and took another swallow.

"Do you hear him, Louis?" Henriette said.

"I am right here, my love."

"Then why don't you say something? Why do you stand there like a lump and not rise to the defense of the woman who has devoted her life to you and given you four wonderful children?"

"After what Monsieur Fargo has just been through, he is entitled to a drink, I think," Louis said.

Henriette glowered at Fargo. "I won't forget this indignity," she snapped, and marched off.

"Sorry," Fargo apologized. "She'll bite your head off later, won't she?"

"She is a good woman," Louis said. "But a little, as you might say, headstrong."

"A little?"

The count glanced over his shoulder, then held out his hand for the bottle. He wiped it on his sleeve and allowed himself a long sip, and handed the bottle back. *"Merci."*

"That's all?" Fargo said.

"It is all I can allow myself, yes." Louis smoothed his jacket. "This is serious business, these attempts on your life. Wouldn't you agree?"

Fargo looked at him.

"Well," Louis said, and coughed, "we must get to the bottom of it."

"Before he kills me," Fargo said.

"I can't imagine why anyone would want you dead," the count said, shaking his head.

"Makes two of us."

"Whoever he is, he might slit your throat in the middle of the night."

"Is this your notion of cheering me up?" Fargo asked, and chuckled.

"I merely voice my thoughts aloud," Louis said. "I happen to be quite fond of you, monsieur. It would upset me greatly if you were to be murdered."

Fargo looked at him again.

"Well, it would," the count said.

9

Lanterns on the front tent poles lit their faces in a yellow glow.

The count was gruff and to the point. One of their number had committed "foul atrocities." They were to form a line and step forward when he beckoned.

Fargo examined each man. He didn't expect the assassin to be among them, and he was right. When the last man had filed past, he said, "This was a waste of our time."

"Was that all of you?" Louis addressed them, and switched to French. Immediately a man stepped forward and they spoke at length. As he listened, Louis's face became as hard as flint.

"Let me guess," Fargo said.

"One of them is missing. His name is Alexandre Sifrein. He was hired in France and sailed with us to America. I regret to say I know no more than that. I've never spoken to the man."

A search was instigated. Half an hour later Claude Dupree reported that Alexandre Sifrein was nowhere in camp, and that one of the horses was missing.

"It's my guess," Claude concluded, "that he has fled to Corpus Christi. We've seen the last of him."

Fargo wasn't so sure. Before he turned in about midnight, he retrieved the ovaro and pounded a picket pin into the ground a few yards from his blankets. The stallion would nicker if anyone came near. Lying back on his saddle with his Colt still strapped around his waist, he placed his Henry across his lap.

The camp lay quiet under the stars. Except for the sentries, the men were asleep. The count and his family had gone to bed hours ago and their tent was dark. So was the smaller tent that belonged to Claude and Odette.

Fargo felt uneasy. He tossed. He turned. He couldn't shake

the feeling that Alexandre was close by, and for whatever reason, would try to finish what he had started.

Eventually, sleep claimed him. But it was fitful. He woke at the slightest sound. Once it was a low whinny from the ovaro. He sat up and searched the night but saw nothing.

Shortly before dawn, as the eastern sky was changing from black to gray, soft footfalls brought Fargo up with the Henry in his hands. "What the hell?" he blurted.

The twins were sneaking from their tent, wearing their nightgowns and robes. They held hands and smiled as they crossed to where he lay, and squatted.

"Bonjour, *beau*," one of them whispered.

"*Comment allez-vous?*" whispered the other.

"English, damn it," Fargo said.

"We are sorry, monsieur," the first one said. "We forgot ourselves."

"Are you Blanche or Jeanne?" Fargo asked.

"Blanche," she replied, and both of them giggled.

"Why are you out here? Your mother will have a fit if she sees you."

"We must talk to you before she is awake," Blanche said.

"*Oui*," Jeanne said. "If we were to talk to you during the day, she would be suspicious."

"She knows us very well," Blanche said.

"But then, her blood is our blood, is it not?" Jeanne said.

They indulged in more giggling.

Fargo was growing tired of their antics. "If you have something to say, say it."

"*Très bien*," Blanche said. "We have drawn lots and Jeanne won. She will be first and I will be second."

"At what?" Fargo asked, with a quick glance at the tent. He thought he'd heard someone moving around in there.

"At you, of course," Jeanne whispered.

"Me? Stop talking in riddles. What is it you want? Come right out with it."

"I should think it obvious," Blanche said.

Jeanne nodded. "We want you."

"Is that a fact?"

"We want to make love to you," Jeanne clarified. "I will have you the first time and Blanche will have you the next."

"You're taking turns?"

They giggled and nudged each other and Blanche said, "You have la reputation as a, how do you say it, a ladies' man?"

"It is rumored you have made love to a great many women," Jeanne said.

"Two or three," Fargo said.

"Oh, it is very many more than that," Blanche said.

Jeanne smiled. "We would like you to add us to your total."

"I'll be damned."

"Please, monsieur. Don't mock us," Blanche said. "We are in earnest. My sister and I, we very much like the sex."

Fargo almost laughed.

"*Oui. Faire l'amour,*" Jeanne whispered. "But our mother always watches us closely. We must behave as perfect ladies or suffer her wrath."

"Ladies," Blanche said, as if it were too horrible to contemplate.

"So we get our men where we can," Jeanne said, "and we want to get you."

"We would have approached you last night but for the incident with the man who tried to kill you," Blanche said.

"We are glad he didn't," Jeanne said. "We both of us think you must look magnificent naked."

Fargo realized he was still pointing his rifle and set it on his lap. "You just come right out with it? Is that how French girls are?"

"If we did not come out with it," Jeanne said, "we would never have any."

"Men, she means," Blanche said. "You would be surprised how hard it is to bed a man unless a woman goes through the ritual of being courted. And we are not interested in romance."

"Not at all," Jeanne said.

"All we want is to . . . how do you Americans say it? Fuck?"

"That's how I say it," Fargo said.

Blanche was about to make a remark when a sound from in the big tent caused them to stiffen. Each touched him on the arm, then quickly rose and hurried in.

"I'll be damned," Fargo said to the swinging flap. There were worse ways to start a day. He rose and stretched.

A sleepy sentry was over by the horse string. Another was at the far end of the camp, leaning on a rifle and yawning.

Fargo needed coffee. The nearest fire had burned low so he rekindled it, refilled the coffeepot, and put the coffee on to brew. Since it would be a while, he saddled the ovaro, shoved the Henry into the scabbard, and climbed on.

The sentry at the horses gave him a quizzical look as he began a circuit of the encampment.

Fargo nodded at him, then devoted his attention to the ground. He was looking for sign. Alexandre Sifrein had stolen a horse, so there might be hoof marks to show which direction he went. Then again, the ground was hard, and they had trampled so much of it when they arrived and were setting up camp, that Fargo wasn't optimistic. He started on the prairie side and had gone halfway around when he drew rein. There, plain as could be, were scuff marks and a partial print made by a single horse that had gone into the woods bordering the Nueces.

"Well, well, well," Fargo said to himself. His would-be killer hadn't gone back to Corpus Christi, after all. The man was out there somewhere, lurking, maybe waiting for another chance.

Fargo glanced toward the fire and the coffeepot—and reined into the trees. He would be damned if he'd be looking over his shoulder the rest of the trek. Better to end it here and now, even if he had to use himself as bait to lure Sifrein out.

The forest was coming alive. Pink bands on the eastern horizon were the signal for every songbird in creation to greet the new day. Squirrels came out of their treetop nests to chatter as if in annoyance at the birds.

A few deer were up and about, eating shoots and buds.

Fargo breathed deep. He loved the wilds as he loved little else in life. Whiskey, poker, women, all came close, but he could only take so much of them and he inevitably returned to his first love.

Fargo came to the river and drew rein. At that time of year the water was low. He saw where a shod horse had gone out on a gravel bar and crossed to the other side.

Gigging the ovaro, he did the same. The tracks led into thick vegetation on the far side. He stopped and cocked his head, listening.

An acrid scent tingled his nose.

Fargo shifted toward camp and sniffed a few times, and then

turned to the vegetation and sniffed a few more. There could be no mistake. The smoke he smelled came from off in the forest.

Dismounting, Fargo tied the reins to a sapling. He shucked the Henry, made sure a round was in the chamber, and stealthily stalked forward, the smell growing stronger with every step.

Surely not, Fargo thought. The man wouldn't be so careless as to stop so close. He reminded himself that Sifrein was alone in a strange land filled with hostiles and savage beasts. Perhaps Sifrein was afraid to stray too far for fear of becoming lost, or worse.

Fargo exercised the caution of an Apache. He was careful not to step on twigs or snap any of the many small branches that poked at his buckskins.

The smoke odor was so strong, he knew it had to be very close. He crept on and suddenly saw orange and red flames dancing low.

Alexandre Sifrein was huddled by the fire drinking from a tin cup and looking miserable. He looked up, and for a few seconds Fargo thought Sifrein was looking at him. But no, the Frenchman was gazing toward the big camp. Sifrein did it several times. Finally the man rose and paced and tapped his foot.

It occurred to Fargo that Sifrein was waiting for someone. That changed everything. Instead of shooting him then and there, Fargo flattened and set the Henry crosswise.

Whoever put Sifrein up to killing him—and Fargo was sure someone had—must be coming to pay the killer a visit.

The Frenchman commenced to pace. Once he stopped to regard the rising sun and then turned toward the big camp and frowned. As he resumed pacing he muttered something in French.

Fargo began to share the man's impatience. He'd like to find out who was behind the attempt on his life, and why.

Suddenly Sifrein stopped and peered into the woods.

Fargo heard them, too: footsteps.

Someone was coming.

10

Alexandre Sifrein moved closer to the trees.

Prone on the ground, Fargo spied a figure in the shadow of a pine. Whoever it was had stopped and was just standing there.

Sifrein beckoned and spoke in French.

The figure didn't move.

Sounding angry, Sifrein said something and again beckoned and took a step.

Fargo wondered why the figure stayed silent. Then it hit him; whoever it was had seen the ovaro and knew he was somewhere nearby. He started to rise and stopped when the figure at last moved. Its arms came up. It was holding something, he couldn't make out what.

Sifrein addressed the person again, this time sounding more confused than angry.

Fargo heard a strange sound, a *pffttt*, and saw Sifrein grab at his throat. Sifrein's eyes went wide and he staggered back.

"*Non!*" Sifrein cried. "*Non! Non! Non!*" And just like that, he collapsed.

The figure whirled and sprinted off.

Pushing up, Fargo gave chase. Sifrein could wait. He needed to know who was behind the attempt on his life. He ran to the pine and scoured the undergrowth, but the woods were still. He started in pursuit anyway, stopping when he came to the ovaro. He still hadn't spotted his quarry.

Whoever it was, they were gone.

With an oath, Fargo climbed on and rode back to the small clearing. Emerging from the trees, he halted in consternation.

Alexandre Sifrein was on his back, his limbs in the grip of convulsions. His mouth was open, and out of it came inarticulate grunts and groans mixed with a bubbling white froth. His eyes were stark with fear. He looked at Fargo and tried to speak but couldn't.

"What the hell?" Fargo vaulted down and dipped to a knee. The only time he'd seen anything like this was when he'd had to shoot a rabid raccoon that was foaming at the mouth, and once when a patent medicine man gave some people medicine that made them violently sick.

Sifrein clutched at Fargo's wrist. His face became as red as a beet and his veins bulged. He was trying to say something, and couldn't.

Only then did Fargo see the feathers sticking out of Alexandre Sifrein's throat. They were white, and had been trimmed so they weren't more than an inch long.

Sifrein made another effort to speak. His face was practically purple. His fingers on Fargo's wrist were a vise. Suddenly he arched his back and went into a long spasm that ended in a loud gasp and complete collapse. His tongue jutted from the froth covering his mouth.

Fargo didn't need to feel for a pulse to know the man was dead. He pried Sifrein's fingers loose. Then, using a thumb and forefinger, he gingerly gripped the ends of the white feathers and tugged.

Out came a small dart. The tip was wood, not metal, and discolored. Not from blood, but from something it had been dipped in. Fargo sniffed it. It had an odor he couldn't place. He was willing to bet every cent in his poke that it was poisoned.

"A damn dart," Fargo said. He'd never seen one like it. The feathers weren't eagle feathers or duck feathers or any other bird he knew.

Fargo placed the dart on Sifrein's chest. If he was right, and Sifrein had been waiting for whoever he was working for, then that was who killed him. On the face of it, it made no sense. Why kill your own killer? Unless, Fargo mused, whoever was behind Sifrein was afraid he'd be caught and talk.

Fargo examined the dart more closely. It was well made. Some sort of animal sinew had been used to tie the feathers to the thin shaft. Whatever poison was used was incredibly potent, much more so than the rattlesnake venom that some tribes used on their arrows.

Abruptly aware that his back was to the woods, Fargo picked

up the Henry and stood. Whoever used the dart on Sifrein might use one on him. Entering the trees, he made his way to the ovaro and climbed on.

A golden crown adorned the rim of the world. The camp was astir, with everyone up and about. Breakfast was being made, and Fargo's stomach growled.

The flaps to the big tent were tied open and servants bustled about. Several were kept busy bringing water for the morning baths for the women.

Fargo drew rein but stayed in the saddle and addressed a male servant about to take water in. "Do you savvy English?"

The servant stopped.

"Fetch the count."

Shaking his head, the servant mimed that he didn't understand.

"The count," Fargo said. "Comte Louis Tristan."

At the name, the servant nodded and hastened in. It wasn't a minute later that the count strolled out, dressed as if about to promenade on a Paris street.

"Monsieur Fargo. *Bonjour.* How are you this fine morning?"

"Pissed," Fargo said. "Are you up for a ride?"

"We are going somewhere?"

"I found Sifrein."

"And you didn't bring him here so I can interrogate him?"

Fargo lowered an arm. "Climb on and I'll take you to him."

"Ride double?" Louis shook his head. "Why do that when I have my own horse?" He clapped his hands and two servants appeared, eager to do his bidding. In short order his mount was brought, already saddled, and one of the servants held the stirrup steady while the count climbed on.

"Wish I had a stirrup holder," Fargo said.

"Do you mock me, sir?"

"You need to see this." Fargo avoided the question. Reining around, he used his spurs.

Louis quickly caught up and together they left the camp and were soon at the river. Fargo crossed first and led the count to the small clearing.

"Mon Dieu!" Louis exclaimed. "Is that the missing man?"

"I said it was." Fargo stayed in the saddle so he could keep one eye on the woods.

Louis knelt, bent over the dead man's chest, and gave a start. He said something in French, then caught himself and switched to English. "What is this I see? Is this how he died? By a pygmy dart?"

"A what?" Fargo said.

Louis pointed at the lethal projectile. "I have seen these before. When we were in Africa. We visited the interior and a delegation from a pygmy village paid us a visit. They were expert with the blowgun and the poison dart." Louis gingerly touched the white feathers. "Do you see these? They come from a giant bird called an ostrich. The pygmies value their feathers above all others and trade all they have for them."

"What the hell is that dart doing here?"

"I do not know," Louis said. "I certainly did not bring a blowgun back with me."

"Who could have? Who else went to Africa with you?"

Louis looked up. "My whole family."

"Henriette?"

"Of course. She is my wife."

"The twins? Your sons?"

"Did you not hear me say my whole family?"

"Claude and Odette?"

The count nodded. "They went, too. They go everywhere we go. My wife and her sister are very close."

"Then it could have been any of them," Fargo said.

Louis blinked and stared at the dart. "My word. You're right. Whoever killed this man had to have been with me in Africa. There is no other explanation."

"One of them wants me dead." Fargo voiced the suspicion he'd held for days now.

"But why, in heaven's name?" Louis said. "What could you have done? It defies all reason."

"Maybe I haven't done anything," Fargo said. "Maybe it's my being here."

"Someone doesn't want you to act as our guide? But why? You came so highly recommended." Louis shook his head in bewilderment. "I admit to being confused."

"You're not the only one."

"Why didn't they simply use the blowgun on you?" Louis wondered.

"Because you'd know it was one of your family," Fargo speculated. "So they hired Alexandre to shoot me or knife me."

"But they used a dart on him," Louis said, with a jab of his thumb at the body. "That gives it away the same as if they used it on you."

"They had no choice," Fargo said. "They knew I'd found him and they needed to shut him up, permanent."

"So he couldn't implicate the guilty party." Louis thoughtfully rubbed his chin. "*Oui.* That makes sense. Only now we are no closer to solving the mystery than before. We have no idea who it is."

"There's something else you should be thinking about," Fargo said.

"Enlighten me, my friend."

"Maybe I'm not the only one they want dead," Fargo said. "Maybe they want me out of the way to have a clear run at you."

"Are you suggesting . . . ?" Louis began, and stopped. "That is preposterous."

"Think about it. Is there any reason any of them would want to bury you?"

"Surely you jest. My own family? My wife and I have been married for almost thirty years. We are very much in love. It couldn't be her."

"There are six more."

"My daughters? Have you not seen how much they adore me? They are too sweet, too innocent."

Fargo recalled how the twins had snuck out to proposition him, and said nothing.

"Blanche and Jeanne could never conceive of so vile a deed. As for Charles and Philip, a father could not ask for two more devoted sons."

"That leaves Odette and Claude."

"I've already told you. My wife and her sister are very close. Odette would never harm me because it would bring great sorrow to Henriette."

"We're down to Claude, then."

Louis opened his mouth to respond, hesitated, and closed it again.

"So, there is one you don't fully trust?"

"Claude is headstrong," Louis said. "He is too belligerent at times."

"Are you and him pards?"

"What? Oh no. We're friendly, but not the best of friends. Even so, I can't think of any reason he would want me dead. Or you."

"Someone sure as hell does," Fargo said.

11

The family took the news of the assassin's death with little show of emotion.

Fargo watched Claude Dupree closely as the count told about finding the body and the dart. The brother-in-law might as well have been carved from stone.

The grand expedition, as Louis kept referring to it, packed up their tents and their effects and loaded the wagons and pushed on.

Fargo scouted ahead. In a few days they would reach a plateau, and he hoped to run into buffalo before then. At that time of year, there were always herds to be found.

He was alert for Indian sign, as well.

It was early afternoon when he found some. He was miles from the river, making his wary way through low, rolling hills, when the ovaro raised its head and sniffed.

Fargo slowed.

Around the next hill was a small spring. The animal sign told him that deer and rabbits and raccoons and an opossum had recently paid the spring a visit. So had coyotes and a fox and a bobcat.

Then there were the moccasin tracks and the hoofprints.

Fargo sank to a knee to study them. He counted five warriors. The impressions weren't clear enough to tell much about the stitching or the cut. Since no friendly tribes lived in that area, it was likely they were either Comanches or Kiowas.

Neither was fond of whites.

Fargo reckoned he would follow the tracks awhile. He let the stallion drink, took off his bandanna, and washed his face and neck free of dust and sweat, and was back in the saddle.

The trail puzzled him. The five warriors had gone east for a while, then north, then west. They appeared to be searching for something. Buffalo, he figured. The sun was well on its dip to the horizon when he reined around and headed for the count's caravan.

It bothered him that the dust the wagons were raising could be seen for miles. The warriors might spot it, too.

The count and his sons were out in front of the column. Louis and Philip greeted him warmly. Charles couldn't care less.

"Indians, you say?" Louis said excitedly on being informed of the tracks. "Are they hostiles, do you think?"

"Odds are," Fargo said.

"We must post extra guards tonight, *oui*? And take special precautions with our horses."

"And with the women," Philip said. "In the stories I've read, savages are always stealing white women to violate them."

Charles snorted. "You and those atrocious tales you are so fond of."

Fargo had met a few other people who read the things. In England they were called penny dreadfuls. To say they were preposterous was putting it mildly. The writers had never been to the West. Some of them had never been to America. They knew no more about Indians than they did about life on Mars. Yet that didn't stop them from concocting the most ridiculous stories. He remembered one where a scout called Dandy Dave slew thirty "heathen redskins" single-handedly with nothing but a small clasp knife. It was too damn silly for words. Clearing his throat, he said, "It's the horses they'll want more than the women."

"Are you certain, monsieur?" Philip asked. "I would hate to think of Mother living the rest of her days in a dirty hovel made of hides."

"We call them lodges or tepees," Fargo said, setting him straight, "and they're cleaner than a lot of homes whites live in."

"You have been in these lodges, I presume?" Louis inquired.

"Many times," Fargo said.

"Clean or filthy, my wife would not fare well in captivity. She is too proud. Too independent."

Fargo didn't mention that few Indians would want her. A lot of tribes thought white women made terrible wives. The

Apaches, in particular, regarded them as weak and next to worthless.

That evening Fargo called a halt in a bend of the Nueces. With the help of a couple of Texans, he rigged a rope corral for the horses. The tents were pitched close to each other in the very middle of the camp so no one could get to them without being seen. Orders were given that the sentries were to keep at least two of the fires burning all night.

Once again Fargo was invited to eat with the aristocrats. The meal was as sumptuous as the last and included fresh venison from a buck one of the drivers had shot during the day.

The family was unusually quiet. Fargo reckoned it was because of the Indians until the usually shy Odette coughed and said in her soft voice, "This business of the dart troubles me."

Everyone stopped eating and looked at her.

"This is hardly the time or the place to bring that up," Claude said darkly, with a bob of his head at Fargo.

Odette surprised Fargo by replying, "I think it is. It is on my mind that the dart could only come from Africa."

The count said, "I have already come to the same conclusion, my dear."

"Then that means . . ." Odette said, and stopped.

"Yes," Louis said. "It had to be one of us."

"With all due respect," Claude said, "that's nonsense. None of us are murderers. And need I remind all of you that our servants were with us in Africa, as were seven or eight of the men currently in our employ?"

"What?" Fargo said.

"It is true, American," Claude said. "We had, as you would say, a small army with us, as a safeguard against attacks by the natives and the depredations of the many beasts. Lions and leopards are much more formidable than any animal you have here."

"Tell that to a griz," Fargo said. He looked at the count. "Why didn't you tell me about the ones who were in Africa with you?"

Louis shrugged. "They are hired help. I didn't think it important."

Fargo swore. It added another twenty people or so to those he had to watch out for. Picking up the table knife, he cut his

58

venison into pieces and forked one into his mouth. He was thinking about the darts and heard Henriette mention his name. "What was that?" he said, looking up.

"I was saying to Louis that this business with Alexandre Sifrein changes everything. I think we should turn back to Corpus Christi. What do you think?"

Louis broke in with "It's what *I* think that counts, and I refuse to let this spoil my dream. We will continue on, and that's that."

Ignoring him, Henriette said, "Monsieur Fargo? I await your opinion."

"Your husband is paying me five thousand dollars," Fargo said. "I go where he goes."

"You see, my dear?" Louis said smugly.

"The money aside, Monsieur Fargo," Henriette persisted. "Do you consider it wise for him to go on?"

"No one is out to kill your husband," Fargo said. "They're out to bury me."

"But why?" one of the twins said. "You have been a perfect gentleman."

"It is insane," said the other.

Charles tapped his plate with his spoon. "May I have a say, Mother?"

"But of course."

Charles shifted toward his father. "I think it very unwise. We have no idea why Sifrein tried to kill the scout or why Sifrein was in turn murdered. Let us embrace common sense and return to Corpus Christi before it is too late."

"Are you quite through?" Louis said indignantly. "It is precisely because we don't know that we *must* push on. I can't speak for Monsieur Fargo, but I, for one, would like to get to the bottom of this."

"Even at the cost of our lives, Father?"

"Oh, please. You mock your brother for his love of dramatic stories, but you indulge in drama yourself. We will be perfectly fine. I've taken every precaution."

"There is no talking to you when you are like this," Claude said. "You refuse to listen to reason."

Fargo was sick of their bickering. He pushed back his chair and stood. "Be seeing you."

"Wait," Henriette said. "What about dessert?"

"I have my own." Fargo touched his hat brim and left. He made straight for his saddlebags, took out his bottle, and treated himself to a long swig. "Ahhh," he said as the whiskey burned his gullet. He admired the stars and smelled the scent of burning wood from the campfires and was about to take another swallow when footsteps shuffled.

"Father sent me to ask if you are all right," Philip said. "He was upset that you left the dinner table so abruptly."

Fargo held out the bottle and Philip shook his head. "Suit yourself." He raised the bottle to his lips.

"I must confess I am troubled," Philip said. "I don't want anything to happen to you."

Fargo crooked an eyebrow.

"Why anyone would care to do you harm is beyond me. You are nothing but our scout."

"Thanks," Fargo said.

"No, that wasn't derogatory," Philip said. "I respect you highly. But killing you serves no purpose."

"Unless someone wants your father to turn back."

"Then they don't know him as I do. He would push on without you. He's that stubborn."

As much as he would like to drink the whole bottle, Fargo capped it and shoved it into his saddlebag. "Go finish your meal."

"Are you sure? I can keep you company."

"I don't want any," Fargo said. He leaned back on his saddle and folded his arms.

"I hope you don't think that I am to blame for any of this," Philip said.

"Of all your family," Fargo assured him, "I trust you the most."

"*Merci, mon ami,*" Philip said with feeling. "I will prove worthy of it. I will watch your back from here on out."

"I don't need a nursemaid."

"I will watch you anyway." Philip smiled and bowed and bent his steps to the big tent.

"Hell," Fargo said. The food and the whiskey had him feeling drowsy. Sinking lower, he pulled his hat brim low over his eyes. He reckoned to rest a bit, then get up and patrol the camp.

But he was more tired than he thought. The next he knew, a hand was on his shoulder, lightly shaking him. Pushing his hat up, he straightened and was flabbergasted to see that the fires had burned low and everyone was asleep.

"It is only me, monsieur," whispered a grinning vision beside him. "Jeanne."

"What do you want?" Fargo asked without thinking.

"Why, to make love to you, of course."

12

Fargo looked at her.

Jeanne had brushed her hair so it was full and lustrous. She wore a robe tied at the neck that covered whatever she had on underneath, which couldn't be much because her breasts thrust out as if trying to burst free. On her feet were pink slippers. She looked as clean and fresh as a spring flower and smelled of expensive perfume. "Did you hear me?"

Fargo gazed about the camp. Three sentries roved the perimeter along the wagons and a fourth stood guard over the horses. "Where?" he said.

"Behind our tent," Jeanne whispered. She clasped his hand and Fargo let her pull him to his feet and followed her between the big tent and the tent that belonged to Claude and Odette. She went round the corner and turned and smiled and licked her lips.

The rear of the tent was in black shadow. No one could see them unless they were right on top of them. But the tent walls were thin.

Fargo pointed at it and whispered, "They'll hear."

"Not if we are quiet, handsome one," Jeanne whispered back. Pressing against him, she playfully nipped his neck and his earlobe.

"Damn," Fargo said. He had to admit, he wanted her. He was already stirring, down low. Cupping her firm buttocks, he pulled her into him and covered her mouth with his. She responded eagerly, ardently, her silken tongue darting out, her breath hot and heavy.

Fargo knew that if the count or countess caught them, there'd be hell to pay. He didn't care. He kneaded Jeanne's bottom and she cooed softly and sought to suck his tongue down her throat.

Reaching up, Fargo undid the tie at her throat. Her robe parted, revealing lacy lingerie that no churchgoing American woman would be caught dead in.

"You like?" Jeanne teased in his ear.

"I like," Fargo growled.

She giggled and kissed his cheek and his chin and his neck. Suddenly her hands were on his manhood. In an instant Fargo was rock hard. She breathed a few words in French and ran her fingers up and down.

A lump formed in Fargo's throat. Sliding a hand between them, he cupped a full breast. He pinched the nipple and she shivered. He pulled on it, hard, and she arched her back, her mouth wide. Swooping his mouth low, he lathered first one tit and then the other.

Jeanne ripped his hair and ground her nether mound against his pole.

Fargo was about to slide his tongue lower when Jeanne tugged to get his attention, and pointed.

A sentry was coming around the circle. He was over near the woods, a good sixty feet away.

Fargo stood perfectly still. So did Jeanne. She was grinning as if this was great fun.

The sentry yawned and hefted his rifle. He was bored. He came even with them and unexpectedly stopped. Stretching, he gazed at the heavens and then into the forest. He wasn't in any hurry to move on.

Jeanne curled Fargo's hair with a fingertip. Smirking, she bit his ear.

"Do you want to be caught?" Fargo whispered.

"Wouldn't that be scandalous?" Jeanne replied, sounding as if she half hoped they would be. "But that would not be fair to Blanche."

"Blanche?" Fargo whispered.

"*Oui*. She has to have her turn. If you and I are caught, Mother would see to it that we never left the tent unless under escort. Blanche would not get to make love to you."

"We wouldn't want that."

"No, monsieur," Jeanne said in all earnestness. "We get so . . . what is the English word? Randy?"

"It's as good as any."

"We like men but we must play the part of ladies," Jeanne

whispered. "It is harder than you might think for us to enjoy a good screw."

Fargo nipped a laugh.

"I am serious. The precautions we must take. Back in France the gardener's son accommodated us, but we had to pay him hundreds of francs to keep quiet about it."

Fargo was watching the sentry. The man was walking on, oh so slowly.

"But what we do is no different than what Mother does."

"What did you say?" Fargo wasn't sure he had understood her right.

"*Notre mère.* Our mother. We spy on her, Blanche and I. We have since we were little. The things we have seen and heard would make Father red with rage."

"It doesn't make you mad?"

"Why would we be upset?" Jeanne said. "In our country everyone has lovers. Men are hungry for women and the women are always hungry for men."

"I should pay it a visit," Fargo said.

"*Oui.* Do that. And you will have more females interested in you than you'll know what to do with."

"That'll be the day."

The sentry was almost out of sight.

"But enough talk, *oui*?" Jeanne said. She cupped her breasts and jiggled them. "Perhaps you would like to take up where you left off?"

"Hussy," Fargo whispered.

"Oh yes. Call me names if you like. Hussy. Slut. Tramp. I like dirty words very much." She giggled. "You can even spank me."

Fargo wished he could. But the noise would bring her family out. He settled for kissing her and kneading her breasts and sliding a hand between her soft thighs.

She parted her legs and he ran a finger along her moist slit.

"Oh yesssssss," Jeanne whispered.

Fargo rubbed her knob. Rising onto her toes, she trembled with release, then placed her forehead on his chest and whispered in French. Switching to English, she whispered, "I love it so much."

"You and me both, girl."

Jeanne's fingers pried at his belt buckle, and his pants.

Fargo lowered his gun belt so it wouldn't make noise. He felt her fingers on his pole, and his own need increased tenfold. She stroked him, knowingly, and took him in her palm, and did things more experienced women would do.

His blood roared in his veins, and it was if he were hot with fever.

Both of them were breathing heavily when Fargo took her by the hips and raised her off the ground. She smiled in anticipation. He touched the tip of his member to her slit and paused.

Jeanne looked into his eyes and whispered almost fiercely, "Do it."

Fargo rammed up and in. She threw her head back and for a few moments he thought she would cry out. Somehow she didn't. Instead she sank her teeth into his shoulder and wrapped her legs around his waist and hooked her ankles behind him.

"I will ride you to exhaustion," Jeanne whispered.

Damned if she didn't, almost, too. Fargo rocked up and in and she pumped up and down for long minutes of raw pleasure. More than five, more than ten, more than he had ever lasted before.

Then they were at the brink and Jeanne went over first. She closed her eyes and her body went into spasms of release. She started to moan and caught herself.

For Fargo it was as it always was. He exploded and kept driving up and in until he was spent and drained. Fatigue washed over him, and he firmed his legs to keep his balance.

Jeanne smiled dreamily and kissed him on the cheek. *"Magnifique."*

Fargo grunted.

"When I tell Blanche, she will want you even more," Jeanne whispered.

"Any time," Fargo said.

Jeanne grinned and nuzzled his neck. "We were right about you. You are like us."

"I have tits?"

Smothering a laugh, Jeanne shook her head. "You are like us in that you like sex."

"Who doesn't?"

"A lot of people. You would be surprised how many. Aunt Odette is an example. I've heard Claude complain that she is not much in bed."

"He tell you at the supper table?"

"*Non*. We overheard him talking to Charles, Blanche and I. We spy on them, too."

"Little minxes," Fargo said.

"And proud to be so," Jeanne whispered. She wriggled. "You can put me down."

Fargo eased her off his hips and held her while she lowered her feet to the ground. She leaned against him and pecked his chin.

"I must sneak back in. Thank you. We are friends now, yes?"

"Was that your notion of shaking someone's hand?"

She giggled, quietly. "When two people have made love, there is a bond between them, *non*?"

"There's sweat," Fargo said.

Jeanne's teeth were white in the darkness. "You are much fun to be with. I will make Blanche so envious, she will rip your clothes off."

"So long as she sews them back together again."

Jeanne bestowed a last kiss on him and darted around toward the front of the tent.

Fargo put himself together. He buckled his gun belt and adjusted the holster, and thought about his bottle. He went around the far side of the smaller tent and crossed to his blankets.

The guard by the horses saw him and gave a little wave.

Fargo nodded.

The ovaro was dozing. Sitting, Fargo brought out the whiskey. He indulged in several swallows, leaned back, and sighed with contentment. It was a good end to the day.

Holding the bottle in his lap, he idly gazed at the sparkling stars and at the crackling fires he had ordered should be kept burning all night, and felt a sense of unease come over him. He tried to shake it off, and couldn't. He scanned the camp, wondering if he had missed something. The three sentries were still patrolling the perimeter. The other horses showed no agitation.

Everything was as it should be.

Then why, Fargo asked himself, was he still uneasy? Sitting

up, he set the bottle aside. He looked behind him. He looked at the tents; both were dark and still. He was about to lie back then when he caught sight of a vague silhouette in the dark space between the tents.

The instant he set eyes on it, there was the *pffttt* of the blow-gun.

13

Fargo threw himself down. Out of the corner of his eye, he glimpsed the pale flash of white feathers and heard the *thunk* of the dart embedding itself in his saddle. He'd drawn his Colt as he dived and he fired twice into the dark space. The silhouette had vanished, but he might get lucky. There was no outcry, no yelp of pain.

Fargo heaved himself upright. Some of the sentries were shouting. He paid them no heed and ran to the gap.

Suddenly he realized how exposed he was, standing backlit by the fires, and he crouched.

A couple of sentries were running toward him.

From inside the tents came voices and commotion.

Taking a gamble, Fargo plunged into the space. He stayed low. At the rear he stopped and warily poked his head out.

Nothing.

Swearing, Fargo straightened. He moved into the open, the Colt's hammer back, his finger around the trigger. He looked under the wagons and in the wagons and into the night beyond.

Nothing.

Letting the hammer down, Fargo twirled the Colt into his holster. As he turned, light flared, and the count and countess and the rest of the family, flanked by sentries and others, came around the big tent.

"Monsieur Fargo!" Louis shouted. "Was it you who fired those shots?"

Fargo nodded.

"What on earth for?" Henriette asked. "It gave us a terrible fright."

"Was it red savages?" Charles wanted to know.

Crooking a finger, Fargo led them to where he had bedded down. He pointed at the dart.

"*Mon Dieu!*" Louis exclaimed. "An attempt was made on your life?"

Squatting, Fargo carefully gripped the feathers and pulled the dart loose. The tip had the same discoloration as the first.

"This is unthinkable," Louis exclaimed. "I won't have it. Do you hear me? I won't have it."

Fargo didn't know whom he was talking to since he was staring at the dart.

"I've hired this man as our scout and I won't have him endangered," Louis continued to rant.

"*Mon cher—*" Henriette tried to cut in, but he curtly gestured her quiet.

Turning in a slow circle to his family and his hired helpers, Louis raised his voice. He addressed them in French. Then, for Fargo's benefit, he repeated what he had said in English. "Whoever is behind this, it must stop. Perhaps some of you know who it is. I am offering a bounty for information. A thousand francs. No, five thousand."

"Louis—" Henriette tried again.

"I will not have my expedition ruined," Louis fumed. "I have looked forward to this too much. Charles, you and your brother will instigate a search. Every wagon. Every pack."

"What are we searching for, Papa?" Philip asked.

"The blowgun, what else?"

Charles said, "But that will be like looking for a needle in a haystack. It is easy to hide something so small."

"You will search anyway. The killer must know that I will leave no stone unturned."

"Very well, Father," Charles said. "As soon as the sun is up—"

"*Non,*" Louis said. "Start the search this very minute. Divide the men in half between you and have them help."

"Honestly, husband," Henriette said.

"I agree with Charles," Claude Dupree said. "It will be a waste of time."

"Who among you has something more important to do?" Louis snapped at him.

"We should go back to sleep or we will all be tired tomorrow," Henriette said.

"A little fatigue never hurt anyone," Louis said angrily. He clapped his hands. "Charles. Philip. Get to it. I will have the cook make extra coffee so all of us can stay awake and alert."

"As always, I bow to your wishes," Henriette said.

Fargo had never seen the count so forceful. It changed his impression of the man. "I appreciate all the bother you're going to for me."

"It is not just for you," Louis said. "This killer is a threat to all of us. He must be weeded out."

"How do you know it's a 'he'?"

"Eh?" Louis pulled his robe tighter. "Are you suggesting my wife or one of my daughters is going around shooting darts at people?"

"You have maids," Fargo reminded him, "and other servants."

Louis gnawed his bottom lip. "I hadn't even considered that. Yes, it could be a woman. Whoever it is, we are left with the same question."

"Why are they doing it?"

Louis nodded. "If we could guess their purpose, we might have a better idea of who."

"Those pygmies you ran into in Africa," Fargo said. "Did all of them use blowguns?"

"*Non*. Some used spears. Some had small bows with tiny arrows. Why do you ask?"

"The ones who were partial to blowguns," Fargo said, "how many darts did they carry around with them?"

Louis shrugged. "As I remember, they kept the darts in small pouches they wore around their necks. The pouches were big enough to hold perhaps ten or twelve." He paused. "I see what you are getting at. You wonder how many darts the killer has."

"It could be ten. It could be a hundred."

"*Non*. That many is unlikely," Louis said. "The poison the pygmies used was hard for them to obtain." Louis did more lip gnawing. "Let's say someone was able to convince a pygmy to part with a pouch. That would give them about a dozen darts." He nodded at the one Fargo was holding. "They've used two. That would leave them ten or so."

"They're not much good at it or they wouldn't have missed me."

"Need I point out that they only have to break the skin so the poison enters your blood?" Louis said. "It is very deadly."

"I saw what happened to Sifrein," Fargo mentioned. He'd be damned if he'd let it happen to him.

"It is a good thing you are a light sleeper, yes?" the count said.

"Light?" Fargo said.

"Yes. That you awoke just as the killer was about to shoot the dart at you."

Fargo thought of Jeanne and managed not to smile.

"You must have been—what is the saying?—born under a lucky star?"

"Something like that," Fargo said.

Henriette had been impatiently listening and tapping her foot. "Are we done out here, husband? I would very much like to go back to sleep."

"*Non,* dear wife," Louis said. "You must conduct a search of your own. You and the girls and Odette, if she is willing."

"What do you mean?"

"The servants," Louis said. "Their bags and their clothes. Go through them. Do not leave a pocket or purse unchecked."

"You're joking."

Louis drew himself up to his full less-than-considerable height. "Do I sound like I am? If so, I apologize. Because I assure you, I have never been more serious. You will take the girls and your sister and you will search our tent from top to bottom and end to end and then you will search the wagon where the servants keep their traveling bags."

"But that could take all night."

"It can take two weeks for all I care," Louis said. "I want the culprit found."

Clearly unhappy, Henriette motioned at her daughters and marched into the big tent.

Jeanne glanced over her shoulder and grinned at Fargo.

"What about me?" Claude asked his in-law. "What can I do?"

"You will search my effects, and those of my two sons."

Claude was shocked. "You jest. I could never presume to invade your privacy."

"It's not an invasion if you're invited," Louis said. "I would check Charles's and Philip's things myself, but I'm their father and it wouldn't be right. For you there is no blame."

"And you want me to search your things, too?"

"I would be unworthy of my privileges and estates if I didn't impose on myself the same standards I impose on others."

"But, Comte Tristan . . ." Claude protested.

Louis waved his hand in dismissal. "Get to it. Should my wife object, inform her she is to bring any complaints to me." He grinned. "Oh. You are to search her effects, as well."

"She won't like that," Claude predicted.

"Am I her husband or her cat?" Louis said. "Impress on her that my will is not to be thwarted in this. Not when the killer could be one of my own flesh and blood."

"Surely you don't believe that?"

"To be frank, I don't know what to believe," Louis said. "The repeated attempts on Monsieur Fargo's life are without rhyme or reason." He gestured at the big tent. "What are you waiting for?"

"*Certainement,*" Claude said. Bowing, he hurried in.

Louis sighed and turned to Fargo. "I have done all I can. Unless you can think of something I have missed?"

"Not at the moment," Fargo said. Kneeling, he opened his saddlebags and took out his spare bandanna. Spreading it flat, he deposited the dart in the middle, then carefully folded the bandanna not once but several times.

Exercising the utmost care, he placed the bandanna in his saddlebag and tied the saddlebag shut.

"*Un moment?*" Louis joked.

"You never know," Fargo said.

"I know I do not like having a murderer in our midst." Louis rubbed his chin. "If we find who it is, I suppose the best thing to do is to bind them and turn them over to the American authorities after we return to Corpus Christi."

"I have a better idea," Fargo said, and patted his Colt.

"You could kill someone in cold blood?" the count asked.

"They're trying to kill me."

"Yes, but still."

"No buts about it," Fargo said.

14

The search turned up nothing.

Everyone was involved, from highest to lowest. It took hours. In the end, all they had to show for their effort was a lack of sleep.

Fargo wasn't surprised. A blowgun and a pouch of darts were small enough to hide most anywhere, even down a sleeve or up a pant leg. And although every trunk, pack, and container was checked, the count wasn't about to have everyone submit to a strip search.

"*Non*," Louis said when Fargo brought it up. "We must preserve a degree of dignity. For me to ask the women to do that would be an insult. Henriette wouldn't stand for it and my girls would be in tears."

Everyone turned in. Fargo was tired and figured he'd drift right off. But his sleep was fitful. He kept dreaming of a dark shape in the night, firing darts at him. Twice he woke up in a cold sweat. The second time, a faint blush of light heralded the new dawn. He was up before the servants and put coffee on to brew. As he hunkered there, waiting, the tent flap parted and out came the brother-in-law.

Claude was dressed in sartorial splendor. His shirt was silk, and he wore a jacket that cost more than most people earned in a year. His knee-high leather boots were polished to a sheen. He stretched and regarded the sky and came over. There was no "good morning." Instead he said grumpily, "All the trouble we went to on your behalf, eh, American?"

"I'm obliged to the count," Fargo said.

Claude held his palms to the fire to warm them. "Louis is too noble for his own good. I could have told him we wouldn't find anything."

"Looked in your crystal ball?"

Claude smiled a thin smile. "You are familiar with the Gypsies, I take it? But no. I did not need the gift of prophesy. Just as I do not need it to predict that there will be more trouble unless you do what is best and leave us."

Fargo imagined how good it would feel to slug him in the mouth. "I missed that part."

"It's obvious," Claude said in unconcealed disdain. "Whoever is out to kill you will undoubtedly try again. The next time, it could be what you would call an innocent bystander who takes a dart, yes?"

"Depends on how good a shot the killer is."

"You make light of me," Claude said. "But if one of us dies, it will be on your head."

"I have an idea," Fargo said. "Why don't you go annoy someone else?"

Claude straightened and scowled. "I don't like you, scout. You are arrogant, and provincial."

"I don't even know what the hell that means."

"It means you do not know your station. In my country a commoner would not address me as you do."

"This is America," Fargo said. "Us commoners talk as we damn well please."

Claude sniffed and wheeled and strode back into the tent.

Fargo was content to squat there sipping coffee and watch the sun rise. When the flap parted again, he turned, but it was Philip.

The youngest son yawned and stretched and smiled. "Good morning, monsieur. What is on our agenda today?"

"Our?" Fargo said.

"*Oui.* My father has charged me with looking out for you. I am to stay by your side every minute until the assassin is caught."

"Like hell you are. I don't need a nursemaid."

"I would agree. But my father has given me the task and I must do as he says."

"Wonderful," Fargo muttered. If it wasn't one thing, it was another.

"So, what do you have planned?" Philip asked.

"Your father wants to shoot a buffalo," Fargo said. "I aim to spend the morning hunting for some."

"Really?" Philip said excitedly. "I have read about them. They are huge, fearsome creatures, are they not? Much like the water buffalo of Africa."

"I've never seen a water buffalo," Fargo said. "I wouldn't know."

"Water buffalo are enormous beasts with short tempers and deadly horns."

"That pretty much describes buffs, too," Fargo said. "It's worth keeping in mind."

"I will be careful, monsieur," Philip assured him. "I have no desire to die."

"No one ever does."

By the time a golden crown blazed the world, the camp was fully astir. Breakfast was served and the teams were hitched and the caravan was ready to get under way.

Fargo left them to forage ahead. He didn't want to take Philip, but the count was bound to argue about it and he could do without the bother.

So, here they were, half a mile ahead of the column, Philip gazing about in wonder at the wilds. "It is a dream come true," he declared happily. "To have read about the West for so long, and to finally be here."

"Do those stories of yours say how dangerous it is?" Fargo asked.

"*Oui*, monsieur. Do not be offended, but your western lands are considered some of the most perilous on the planet."

"It's worth keeping in mind," Fargo said again.

Ahead stretched a vast expanse of rolling prairie. A slight breeze stirred the grass. Here and there were splashes of color: wildflowers. Butterflies flitted and hawks soared and once a rabbit bounded away.

At that time of year, buffalo were farther south than usual, and Fargo was confident it wouldn't be long before they came across some. Sure enough, along about the middle of the morning, brown dots appeared in the distance to the northwest.

"There," Fargo said, and pointed.

Philip rose in his stirrups and laughed in delight. "From this far away they do not look so formidable."

"Up close they're formidable as hell," Fargo told him.

He slowed and circled wide. All together he counted thirty of the brutes. Since he didn't see any calves, he suspected it was a small herd of males.

"Why don't we get closer?" Philip asked.

"We don't want to spook them." Satisfied the herd would graze awhile, Fargo reined around. "Let's fetch your pa."

The wagons were raising a lot of dust. Fargo had been alert for sign of a war party, but so far their luck was holding.

Louis greeted the news of the buffs with enthusiasm. "To finally hunt one of the animals! I will have the wagons stop and we will be ready to go with you in half an hour."

"We?" Fargo said.

"Why, yes. My family is coming. They want to witness the shoot."

"The women, too?"

Henriette, who was listening, broke in with "But of course. Why shouldn't we share in the thrill?"

Fargo figured it would be safe enough so long as they kept their distance, so he didn't object.

It took more than half an hour. The big tent had to be put up. Henriette and Blanche and Jeanne were in there awhile, and when they emerged, they'd changed into whole new clothes.

"Their hunting outfits," Louis said when Fargo remarked that they could have kept on the dresses they were wearing.

"They bought those just to go after buffs?"

"*Oui*, monsieur. My wife has clothes for every occasion. You should have seen the outfit she wore to go rhino hunting."

Some of the men were bringing saddled horses and others over. Twenty, all told.

"Hold on," Fargo said. "Why so many?"

"For us and our servants," Henriette said. "You can't expect us to go anywhere without them."

"Why don't we just take everybody?" Fargo said.

"What is the problem?" Henriette asked. "I take my domestics everywhere."

"Someone must see to our menial needs." Claude threw in his two bits.

"Or do you expect us to make our own tea?" Henriette said sarcastically.

The count was opening an engraved rifle case. Taking the rifle out, he patted it and handed it to his manservant. "He will keep it ready for me to use," he explained.

If Fargo lived to be a hundred, he'd never savvy how some folks would rather be waited on hand and foot than do things themselves.

Finally they were set: the family, five of their servants, and four men who were to handle the packhorses as well as skin the buffalo and preserve the hide.

The wagons would follow at their own pace.

Louis brought his mount next to the ovaro and grinned. "Lead the way, monsieur. I'm eager to vanquish one of these beasts."

Reminding himself that he was being paid five thousand dollars, Fargo gigged the ovaro.

"So, tell me," Louis said. "How do you suggest I proceed once we're there?"

"Stay well back," Fargo said, "and drop one in its tracks."

"Well back?" Louis said. "Where is the sport in that? I prefer to get as close as I can before I squeeze the trigger."

"Any of those buffs catch wind of you," Fargo said, "it'll be you or them."

"Which is exactly how I want it to be," Louis said. "I ask you again. Where is the challenge in shooting from far off?"

"It's safer."

Louis looked at him. "Are all frontiersmen as timid as you?"

"Most like breathing," Fargo said.

The herd had drifted to the west. Fargo raised an arm when they were a quarter of a mile out. "This is as far as the others go. I'll take you a little closer, but only you."

"As you wish," Louis said. He didn't sound pleased about it.

Henriette rode up, flanked by her daughters and her sister. She was riding sidesaddle and held a parasol. "Why have we stopped? This won't do at all. We won't be able to see what happens."

"Monsieur Fargo says it is not wise for you to go any closer, my dear," Louis said.

Henriette stared off at the buffalo. "Be reasonable, husband. I can hardly make them out."

"*Oui, Papa*," one of the twins said. "We want to see every detail."

"You heard them," Louis said to Fargo.

"You don't care if any of them are gored?"

Henriette said something in French, then switched to English. "Your melodramatics, scout, grow tiresome. Kindly take us closer or we will go ourselves."

"It's your funerals, lady," Fargo said.

15

Henriette had brought camp stools and a small folding table. She had the servants set them up on a grassy spine about three hundred yards from the herd. Everything was done quietly. A small fire had been kindled with dry grass for fuel and a pot put on for tea.

Since the wind was blowing from the northwest and the spine was to the southeast, the herd hadn't caught their scent. Fargo couldn't help reflecting that if the wind changed, there'd be hell to pay.

Louis was fondling his rifle. "I had it made to my specifications," he said as he ran his hand along the barrel. "It's powerful enough to drop one of those monsters with a single shot."

Fargo had seen Sharps rifles do the same. This one, though, was a lot fancier. The stock and the grip were etched with flowery designs, and the barrel had been engraved with the family crest. If it could shoot as good as it looked, it was some weapon.

The cartridges were three times the size of the Henry's. The count inserted one into the chamber and gave the rifle an affectionate pat. "I can't wait."

"May I go with you, Father?" Philip requested.

"Alas, my son, you cannot. You must stay with your brother and uncle and protect the women."

"As you wish."

Claude Dupree said, "With all due respect, it shouldn't require all of us."

"Do as I say." Louis rose and shouldered the rifle and moved to his horse. "I am ready when you are, Monsieur Fargo."

Most of the buffalo were grazing, their heads down, their tails lazily swishing. A few had curled their legs under them and were resting. A large bull rolled in a wallow.

"Magnificent!" Louis marveled as they slowly approached.

The word Fargo would have used was *deadly*. Bulls stood more than six feet high at the hump and some were over eleven feet from the tip of their nose to the end of their tail. The heaviest weighed close to a ton. Add to that a set of curved horns with a spread of nearly two feet, and they were death on hooves.

At two hundred and fifty, Fargo glanced at the count and Louis shook his head. At two hundred yards Fargo looked at him again.

"Not yet."

"Damn it," Fargo said.

"The closer, the better."

By Fargo's reckoning they were too close already. He'd seen buffalo hunters drop a buff from half a mile with a Sharps.

"I wonder how close they will let us come," Louis said breathlessly.

At a hundred and fifty yards, Fargo drew rein. "This is as far as you go."

"Non," Louis said, and kept going.

Flaring with anger, Fargo jabbed his heels and reined in beside him. "You don't have to be a sharpshooter to hit one from here."

His rapt gaze on the bison, Louis licked his lips and said quietly, "I like to see the blood."

"You what?"

"The blood, monsieur. I like to see the bullet hit. It gives me great satisfaction."

Fargo began to think the man was loco. "You'd have to be right on top of them."

"Oui. As I was with the water buffalo in Africa. And the hippopotamus. And the rhinoceros. I would have shot an elephant as well, but they are surprisingly elusive for being so immense."

They were a little more than a hundred yards out when a bull raised its head and stared. As if it were a signal, so did several others.

"They've seen us." Fargo stated the obvious.

Louis didn't stop.

"I can't protect you if you get any closer." Fargo tried a last gambit.

"Please, monsieur. Am I an infant?" Louis chuckled. "Everything will be fine. Wait and see." He fondled his expensive rifle as if it were a lover.

"God, when will I learn?" Fargo said to himself.

A large bull had turned and snorted and now it pawed the ground.

"Look at them!" the count exclaimed.

Fargo *was* looking. Almost all of them had stopped grazing. "They can move fast when they want to."

"Be at ease," Louis said.

The large bull did more pawing and tossed its head, a sure sign that it was agitated.

"Count, damn it," Fargo said.

Louis smiled and waved a hand.

They were at a hundred yards. Fargo was tempted to grab the count's reins and get the hell out of there. "I won't be held to blame if this goes wrong."

"Nor will you be." Louis slowed. "Soon," he said. "Very soon."

All the buffalo had their heads up. Several moved toward the horses. They appeared to be more curious than anything, but that could change in an instant.

At last Louis stopped, turning his mount broadside. Shifting in the saddle, he said, "Which to choose? Which do you suggest?"

"The closest," Fargo said.

"It's smaller than some of the others," Louis said. "I would like a big one."

As if in answer to his need, the large bull rumbled and took a few lumbering steps in their direction.

"That one," Fargo said, pointing. "Now."

Louis placed his cheek to his rifle and carefully aimed but didn't shoot.

"What are you waiting for?"

"The blood, remember?"

The large bull was out in front of the others. The rest stopped but not the large one. It advanced, shaking its huge head, its horns glinting in the sunlight.

"If you don't shoot," Fargo warned, "it will come after you."

"Wouldn't that be something?"

Fargo was set to curse a mean streak. If he'd known how foolish the count could be, he'd never have agreed to act as their guide. He opened his mouth to warn him one last time, but it was too late.

The large buffalo charged.

Louis took aim. To his credit, he showed no fear as the living dreadnought bore down on him with the power and speed of a locomotive. He steadied, and when the buffalo had cut the distance by fifty yards, he fired.

The bull didn't even slow.

Louis jerked his head up and hurriedly began to reload. His expensive French rifle was a single shot, and he had to take a new cartridge from a pouch at his side and insert it. He took aim again.

Barely thirty yards separated them.

The buff's hooves pounded like hammers and its head bobbed with every loping stride. Its heavy breaths sounded like a blacksmith's bellows.

Louis fired again.

This time the large bull stumbled, but it didn't go down. Almost instantly, it recovered, and uttering a bellow of pure rage, it bore down on them.

Realizing his plight, Louis frantically fumbled at his pouch.

By then Fargo had the Henry out. He aimed and fired and worked the lever and fired again and then a third and a fourth and a fifth time, shooting as fast as he could, slamming as many of the sixteen rounds as he could into that tremendous bulk in a bid to avert catastrophe.

The buffalo absorbed the leaden hail as if the slugs were snowflakes.

Louis had another cartridge out, but he couldn't seem to slide it in the chamber.

"Get out of here!" Fargo hollered, even as he fired one more time.

Belatedly, Louis clutched at his reins. He gaped at the moving mountain of muscle and hair almost on top of him, and cried out.

The bull rammed into the count's horse. The animal squealed as it was bowled over. Blood sprayed, and its belly was opened wide.

Louis tried to push clear. He cried out again as his horse crashed down, pinning his leg under it.

The bull drew back, tilted its head, and rammed into the thrashing horse a second time. A loop of intestines caught on its horn.

Fargo gigged the ovaro to get around the fallen horse for a better shot. He fired into the bull's side. He fired again.

The bull looked up. Bellowing, it came after him, its short legs churning, clods of earth flying in its wake.

Hauling on the reins, Fargo raced for his life, and the ovaro's. Over short distances buffalo were as fast as horses, and this bull was faster than most. It was almost on them as the ovaro broke into a gallop.

Fargo glanced back and saw horns on either side of the stallion's flank. He jabbed his spurs harder than he ever had.

For harrowing seconds the issue was in doubt. Twice the buff swung its head and nearly hooked the ovaro's rear legs.

It was the stallion's stamina that told. Buffalo were fast, but they lacked endurance. The bull soon slowed and tossed its horns in frustration.

Fargo went on until he saw the bull stop. Drawing rein, he wheeled around.

The count was still pinned and struggling to get free.

Over at the rise, the family were on their feet. The women were yelling, asking if Louis was all right. Charles and Claude had run to their horses and were climbing on.

The commotion caught the bull's attention. It turned and pawed the earth.

"God, no," Fargo said.

The bull launched itself at them.

One again Fargo used his spurs.

Oblivious of their peril, the women continued to holler. The twins were jumping up and down and waving their arms.

Oozing blood from a dozen wounds, the bull thundered down on them.

Philip was by his mother, and he was the first to wake up to their danger and resort to his rifle.

It had no effect.

Charles and Claude were pulling their rifles from their scabbards. Claude unlimbered his first and snapped off a hasty shot. Either he missed, or it, too, had no effect.

The women stopped shouting. Henriette raised her hands to her mouth in horror. Blanche and Jeanne appeared frozen in fear. Odette moved toward the horses.

"Run!" Fargo practically shrieked. "Get the hell out of there!"

Philip was reloading.

Charles fired, in vain.

Fargo was too far away to do any good. He kept hoping the buffalo would drop in its tracks, but it didn't.

And then it was on them.

16

Claude managed to rein out of harm's way. Charles was too slow. The buffalo slammed into his horse and it went down with a crash, spilling him from the saddle. He pushed to his feet, his face twisted in fear, but the bull had veered toward the stools—and the women and his brother.

Philip had his rifle up and got off another shot just as the behemoth reached him. Both twins screamed as their brother went flying.

The bull veered again, into Odette. She had stopped and was rooted in terror. She flung out her hands just as a horn caught her low in the belly. The impact lifted her off her feet and she was tossed like a rag doll.

The bull came to a stop but only for a moment.

The twins were still screaming and it spun toward them, and pawed.

Fargo fired on the fly, worked the lever, aimed, and fired again.

Charles fired.

Off on the plain, Louis fired.

The bull took a step, and swayed. It took another, and tottered. Suddenly it collapsed and rolled onto its side.

Fargo was out of the saddle before the ovaro came to a stop. He ran to the bull and jammed the Henry's muzzle against the brute's eye and fired one last time.

Odette was in the grip of convulsions. Her stomach was a ruined cavity oozing blood and fluids and organs. She gasped, reached up toward the sky as if for succor, and died.

Henriette ran to her sister and stood over her with the strangest expression on her face.

Blanche and Jeanne were hugging each other, overjoyed at their deliverance.

Philip was getting to his feet and holding his left arm.

"Are you all right?" Fargo called to him.

Nodding, Philip limped over.

The servants and the hired men, who had been on the other side of the rise, were rushing to help.

Out of habit Fargo began to reload. He looked at Odette without feeling much of anything. Why should he, when he hardly knew her?

"My sister," Henriette said. "My sweet sister." Sinking to her knees, she clasped her dead sibling's hand.

A shout reminded Fargo that the count was still pinned. He quickly remounted.

The other buffalo were rapidly disappearing to the south.

Louis was frantically pushing against his saddle and tugging at his trapped leg. "My family!" he cried as Fargo came to a stop. "I must get to them!"

Sliding the Henry into the scabbard, Fargo climbed down. He pushed against the fallen horse's saddle, but he might as well be trying to push solid rock.

"Here," Louis said. "I will help."

They pushed together with the same result.

"Hold on," Fargo said. He climbed on the ovaro, and with his rope in hand, rode around to the other side. A flick of his wrist, and he dallied the loop over the saddle horn. He made several loops around his own saddle horn and pulled on the reins to get the stallion to back away.

The rope grew taut. "Be ready," he said.

Louis nodded, then looked at him. "You were right," he said, his voice breaking. "I am sorry."

"Time for that later."

The ovaro strained, the rope held, and inch by slow inch the other saddle came off the ground.

With a desperate wrench, Louis was free. Standing unsteadily, he made for the rise. In his haste he left his rifle.

Fargo dismounted, coiled his rope, and picked the rifle up. He scanned the prairie to be sure all the buffalo were gone, climbed back on, and quickly caught up. "Climb on behind me," he offered.

"*Merci*," the count said. "I am grateful."

Claude was on his knees, cradling Odette's head in his lap. The twins were crying. Tears streaked Philip's cheeks, but Charles showed no more emotion than an adobe brick.

Henriette was staring sadly down at her sister. Louis jumped down, went to her, and tenderly embraced her. She gave him a look that suggested to Fargo that she didn't want to be held.

As for the servants and the rest, they stood silent, their heads bowed in respect.

Fargo stayed apart, and in the saddle. Someone had to keep an eye out for threats.

It must have been a quarter of an hour later that the count came over and said softly, "I should have listened to you."

"You sure as hell should have," Fargo agreed.

"They are far more nimble than water buffalo, these bison of yours," Louis said. "I did not think anything so big could move so fast."

"Just so you know," Fargo said, "grizzlies can move fast, too."

Louis stared at the ring of sorrowful souls. "My brother-in-law will never forgive me. To say nothing of my wife." He took a ragged breath. "I can never forgive myself."

"We all make mistakes."

Louis managed a wan smile. "How incredibly kind of you. But no, there is no excuse. I was willful and stupid and poor Odette has paid the price."

"It could have been worse."

"*Oui*," Louis said, and shuddered. "More of them could have died."

"Will you turn back to Corpus Christi?" Fargo asked.

"That would be wisest, would it not?" Louis said. "I don't want the lives of more of my loved ones on my hands."

"We will do no such thing, husband," Henriette said angrily, coming down the short slope. "To turn back now would make Odette's death meaningless. We will push on with this expedition of yours, come what may."

"Henriette—" Louis tried to respond.

His wife held up her hand. "For once you will listen to me. I have just lost my sister to your folly. She was as near and dear to me as life itself. I will not have you disgrace her memory and her sacrifice by abandoning this grand adventure of yours."

"You're serious?" the count said.

"Never more so," Henriette assured him. "In fact, if you turn back, the rest of us will go on without you."

"That's silly."

Claude appeared, the front of his shirt stained with his wife's blood. "I agree with Henriette, Comte Tristan. Odette would not want you to give up on her account. She was so pleased that at last your dream of visiting the American West had come true."

"She was?"

"For my sake and my wife's as well as Henriette's, don't cut your adventure short."

"I don't know," Louis said uncertainly.

It was plain to Fargo that the count had already given in but wasn't willing to admit it. To get their attention he cleared his throat. "We should send someone for a wagon."

"A wagon, monsieur?" Henriette said.

"Unless you aim to bury your sister here or throw her over a horse to take her back."

"Oh no, that would be shameful," Henriette said. "Thank you for bringing it to our attention." She paused. "I would rather Odette was buried near the river. It is more scenic. How about you, Claude?"

"Whatever you wish, my dear."

Henriette gave him a sharp look, then said, "Very well. The river it is. Unless you object to doing so, my husband?"

Louis, deep in thought, shook his head. "As Claude says, whatever you wish. I have caused enough hurt for one day and do not care to inadvertently cause more."

Fargo stayed with the family while two riders went for a wagon. After they'd reverently wrapped the body in a blanket and placed it in the bed, he escorted them to where the column had made camp along the Nueces River.

While Louis and his loved ones conferred in their tent about how to conduct the funeral, Fargo sat by the fire, drinking coffee. He figured he would be left on his own the rest of the day, but Philip limped out and came to the fire and slowly sat.

"How are you holding up?" Fargo asked.

"My left arm is still numb and my left ankle is sprained and I hurt all over, but otherwise I am fine," Philip said with a rueful grin.

"You were damned lucky."

"I know." Philip touched his left ankle, and winced. "That could well be me in a burial shroud and not sweet Odette."

"Do you want your father to go on like the others do?" Fargo asked.

"No," Philip answered. "Frankly, I am surprised Mother does. The sister she loved so much has died. I should think she would be crushed and wish to return to France."

"How are your sisters?" Fargo had an ulterior motive for wanting to know; Blanche still had to have her turn at making love to him.

"Despondent," Philip said. "They, too, loved Odette very much. It will be days before they are themselves again."

"I'm sorry to hear that."

"I came out to ask you about something else," Philip said. "Should we go back to skin that buffalo now or will it keep until after Odette is buried?"

The family, Louis in particular, had forgotten about the bull, overcome as they were with grief. Fargo had thought about mentioning it, but hadn't. "You want the buff's hide?"

"Father did. He had his heart set on having it stuffed and mounted. But he can't leave Mother's side at a time like this, so I will see to it for him. We can take a wagon or use packhorses. Which would you suggest?"

Fargo would rather not sit around watching the twins whimper and sniffle and the rest act as if the world had come to an end. "A wagon."

"I will see to it."

So it was that presently Fargo found himself riding next to one as it creaked and rattled. Two men were perched on the seat. In the bed was a third, along with skinning knives and a tarp and ropes.

Philip was on the other side of the wagon, but now he came around. He'd been unusually quiet since they left camp, and broke his silence with "I have been thinking about Aunt Odette. She never wanted to come, but Mother forced her to."

"She didn't?"

"Odette was scared to death of the red savages. They gave her nightmares, she said. But Mother wouldn't hear of her staying home. They always went everywhere together."

"Do you blame your mother for her death?"

"*Je n'aurais jamais.* I would never. No one is at fault, not even Papa. It happened, and that is that."

Black dots were circling high in the sky.

"Buzzards," Fargo said, and gestured. "We're almost there."

"Will they spoil the hide? My father will be most unset if it is ruined."

"It depends on how much of the bull they've eaten," Fargo said.

Philip frowned and gazed about them. "This wilderness of yours can be most cruel."

"You don't know the half of it."

17

The rise swarmed with black carrion eaters.

Fargo tapped his spurs and brought the ovaro to a gallop. He let out an Apache war whoop and most took wing. They were slow and ponderous getting off the ground, but as they climbed they gained strength and speed. Scores were above him when he reached the carcass.

The buzzards had pecked out the eyes and eaten some of the nose and the tongue—they liked to go for the soft parts first—and had started to tear open the belly, but otherwise the hide was almost intact.

A few stubborn vultures had hopped off and were waddling about and hissing.

Dismounting, Fargo ran at one and kicked it. The big bird lurched into the air and the rest did the same. One nearly clipped him with its wing.

The wagon was still a few hundred feet away. Fargo sat on the bull to wait. He was tempted to take a drink, but he only had half the bottle left and needed it to last until the "expedition" was over. Sighing, he placed his hands on the buff and leaned back. He idly scanned the prairie, and stiffened.

Far to the north sat several riders.

Jumping up, Fargo moved around the bull for a better look. They were Indians. That much was obvious. But he couldn't tell which tribe. "Damn."

Fargo went to the ovaro and swung on. He gigged the stallion to the north at a fast walk. He'd covered half the distance and was still too far away to identify them when the three reined around and galloped off.

Fargo didn't go after them. It would be a fool's gambit.

Instead, he drew rein and watched until they were out of sight, and headed back.

Philip and the men from the wagon had begun to cut on the bull.

"Where did you get to, monsieur?" Philip asked. "Why did you hurry off like that?"

"You didn't see them?"

"See who?"

Fargo sighed. It had been his experience that greenhorns were about as observant as tree stumps. He told him about the warriors.

"Comanches, do you think?" Philip asked anxiously.

"Or Kiowas." Which was almost as bad, Fargo reflected. The Kiowas weren't any more fond of the invading whites than the Comanches.

"It isn't good that they saw you, *est-il*?"

"Not good at all," Fargo said. He slid down. "We'd best get this over with as quickly as we can." If a war party showed up while they were in the middle of carving on the buff, they might have to fight for their lives.

They set to work. Fargo had skinned his share of buffs, and oversaw the peeling. He'd never worked as a hide hunter, though, men who went around killing buffs by the hundreds and taking the hides but leaving the rest to rot. It always struck him as a terrible waste. A lot of tribes felt the same, and were incensed about it, the Dakotas, or the Sioux, as they were called, in particular. The buffalo was their way of life. They depended on the great herds for nearly everything, from the lodges they lived in down to their sewing needles. Fargo was of the opinion that in coming years their anger would rise to rage, and a lot of blood would be spilled.

There was a technique to peeling a hide. If not done right, a hide was useless.

They started by rolling the bull onto its back. Fargo used a skinning knife to slit down each hind leg and cut along the middle of the belly from the tail to the chin. He slit the inside of the front legs, and was ready to commence with the peeling. It was a slow process.

Philip and the others helped, Philip scrunching his face in distaste at the hairless flesh.

To take the hide off intact was only the first step. In cold weather it could be set aside for a while, but not in hot weather when the flies could get to it. Fargo and Philip stretched it out flat, the hair side down, and proceeded to salt it using bags the count had bought for that purpose in Corpus Christi. The salt had to be rubbed in, not sprinkled, which was rough on the hands.

After an hour or so, the job was done. They carried the hide to the wagon and placed it in the bed.

"I smell awful," Philip said, sniffing his hands. "When we get back I need a bath."

"A little stink never hurt anybody," Fargo remarked.

"You say that, monsieur," Philip responded, "but I have noticed you are not like a lot of your countrymen."

"I'm not?" Fargo said.

"*Non*. Too many of them, I am sad to say, stink. You evidently wash now and then."

It was true that a lot of folks regarded baths as bad for the health and only took one or two a year. Fargo used a washbasin every day when he was in a town and washed in rivers, streams, and springs when he was on the trail.

"In France we place a greater value on hygiene," Philip was saying.

The men climbed onto the wagon to depart. Suddenly the driver pointed and exclaimed, "*Regarde par la!*"

Fargo had a hunch what he would see before he turned.

The three Indians had become seven. They were a mile off, maybe more, sitting their horses, watching.

"Do we go to them?" Philip asked.

"We do not."

"Why?"

"One of us isn't hankering to be a pincushion," Fargo said.

"Perhaps they are friendly."

"And maybe the moon is made of cheese."

"You're that sure?"

"Friendlies," Fargo said, "would ride up and ask for some meat."

"Speaking of which, do we take it back with us?"

Fargo would like to. He could go for a thick slab of juicy buffalo steak. But carving the buff up would delay them from reaching camp until well after nightfall. "Have your men cut off a haunch. The rest we'll leave." He stayed in the saddle and scoured the prairie for sign of more warriors.

Soon the haunch was in the bed with the hide, and the wagon rolled into motion.

Philip rose in his stirrups and waved at the Indians, then gestured at what was left of the buff.

"What in hell are you doing?" Fargo asked.

"Letting them know the meat is theirs if they want it," Philip said. "It doesn't hurt to show them we mean them no harm, yes?"

Fargo doubted the meat would make a difference to Comanches.

The wagon moved so terribly slow that Fargo chafed at the pace. And to the north, the warriors paralleled it, always at the same distance.

Philip kept looking at them. Finally he reined over alongside the ovaro and said, "You know, my friend, I start to see the appeal this land has for you."

"You do, huh?"

"*Oui.* You like the excitement. The living on the edge. Is that not so?"

Fargo was about to say he was full of hogwash. But the truth was, he did like life in the wild, more than anything. And yes, living on the edge, as Philip put it, made him feel more alive than, say, working as a clerk or a bank teller, where the worst that could happen was to stub a toe.

"I don't think it is for me, though," Philip went on. "I like a pleasant existence. A peaceful life. I most especially like not having to worry if I will live through the day."

Fargo chuckled. "There's that."

"I wonder who it is," Philip said.

"Who what?" Fargo thought he was talking about the Indians.

"Who it was that tried to stick a dart in you."

Fargo had been so busy, he'd almost forgotten about the assassin. Once they were back in camp, he'd have to watch his back. Literally. "Thanks for reminding me," he grumbled.

"Monsieurs!" the driver cried, and pointed again.

The seven warriors were now ten.

"Am I right in thinking that is not good?" Philip asked.

"Right as rain," Fargo confirmed.

It seemed to take forever to reach the Nueces. The sun was

less than an hour shy of setting when they arrived. Campfires had been lit and the wagons were arranged in a half circle facing the open prairie, as Fargo had instructed them.

Everyone was gathered in front of the big tent, the men with their hats off and their heads bowed as if they were in church.

Flanked by Henriette and Claude, the count was addressing them. To one side were Charles and the twins.

Louis raised an arm and called out, "Philip! You are back just in time. We are about to begin the funeral. We needed to start to have it done by dark."

Fargo frowned. He rode around the servants and the men and drew rein. "I thought you'd have her planted by now."

"My sister is not a seed, monsieur," Henriette said in contempt.

"We waited as long as we could for Philip's sake," Louis said. "He is part of the family, after all."

"Get it over with quick," Fargo advised.

"How dare you?" Henriette said. "My sister deserves a dignified burial. We will not rush so important a duty."

"He must be impatient for his supper," Claude Dupree said.

Louis was more polite. "Give us a reason why we should hurry so."

Fargo told them about the Indians, and being shadowed all the way back. "I'd bet my poke that they're hostiles," he concluded.

"There are only ten, though, you say?"

Fargo nodded.

"We outnumber them too greatly for them to attack us, don't you think?"

"They decide they want your scalps, that won't matter."

"So they might attack us at any time?" Louis nodded. "Yes. I see the need to hasten things. And to be very much on our guard."

Henriette's face was hard as flint. "I refuse to be intimidated by a few red savages. We will conduct the funeral as we would if they were not around."

"Lady, don't you give a damn if they put an arrow into you?" Fargo said.

Henriette smiled in mock sweetness. "Just so they put one into you, too."

18

As a concession to Fargo, the count posted sentries, which annoyed Henriette. She insisted that everyone attend the burial.

The spot Henriette picked was in a bend of the river, close to the water. When Fargo suggested that it would be better to bury Odette on higher ground, Henriette informed him that Odette was *her* sister and she knew what was best.

Fargo shrugged and walked away. He didn't mention that in the spring, when the heavy rains came, the Nueces would flood and the grave and the remains would be washed away.

Over the next hour he prowled the forest and didn't spot a single hostile. Most would take that as a good sign. He didn't.

The clearing was nearly deserted when he returned. Everyone else was still at the river. He went to a fire and poured himself some coffee. He had hunkered and was taking his first sip when one of the sentries came running up and gestured excitedly while spouting French.

"I don't savvy your lingo," Fargo told him.

The man stamped a foot in irritation and his brow furrowed as if he was trying to remember something. "Come!" he cried in English. "Come! Come! Come!"

Fargo had a sinking feeling as he followed the Frenchman to the end of the wagons. He tried to recollect the man's name and thought it might be Bertrand.

Bertrand stopped and pointed at the ground and said something in French, sounding horrified.

"Hell," Fargo said.

There was blood, a lot of it. Splotches of scarlet led into the vegetation.

Fargo scoured the greenery, then squatted to read the sign. Boot prints showed where a sentry had been standing, and the partial heel of a moccasin revealed that a warrior had snuck up on him from behind. Fargo suspected the warrior had slit the sentry's throat. Drag marks told him where the body had gone.

"Hell," Fargo said again. He glanced at Bertrand. "Fetch the count, pronto."

"*Desole?*" Bertrand said.

"Fetch the count," Fargo said. "Comte Tristan." He wagged his fingers to imitate legs moving fast. "*Rapide.*" He remembered the French word for "fast."

Bertrand nodded and raced toward the river.

Fargo was surprised the war party was so brazen. Usually they'd wait until the whites were off guard to strike. He figured that the sentry's rifle and pistol had been too much of a temptation.

It took god-awful long for Louis to get there. "What is it?" he asked impatiently as he came around the wagon with Bertrand. "What is so important that I had to be called away before—" He stopped. He'd seen the blood.

"*Mon Dieu.*"

"Get everyone into the circle," Fargo said. "Arm all the men."

"*Oui.*" Louis turned, but stopped. "Do you think they will attack in force?"

"No telling."

"If they do, when?"

"When they damn well feel like it."

Louis swallowed, and jogged off.

"Go with him," Fargo said to Bertrand, and gestured to make his point.

Bertrand nodded and did.

Fargo moved around the wagon so it was between him and the woods. The warriors were bound to be watching. They'd see that he was the only one in buckskins and might know enough about white ways to guess that he was guiding the rest, and try to put an arrow into him.

A commotion broke out by the river. Henriette was arguing with Louis.

"Bitch," Fargo said under his breath. He never could understand why some men stayed married to women like her.

He'd as soon go running naked through cactus as be nagged at and argued with day in and day out.

Philip and Charles broke from the rest and hurried over,

Philip eagerly, Charles less so. "Mother wouldn't let Father come, so he sent us," the younger man declared. "We are at your disposal."

"If you want my advice—" Charles began.

"I don't," Fargo said. "It's worthless."

"You haven't heard it yet," Charles said indignantly. "I was about to advise that we pack everything and head for Corpus Christi. The savages will not bother us if we go."

"Lived with a lot of Indians, have you?" Fargo said.

"Live in a dwelling made from animal skins? With primitives who run around half-naked? And are filthy with lice and fleas?"

"They're people, not dogs," Fargo said.

"They're animals. I would no more live with them than I would with cows."

Philip asked, "What do we do?"

"Despicable, ignorant animals." Charles wouldn't stop. "Just like those blacks in Africa. With their silly superstitions and their barbaric ways."

"Are you done?" Fargo said, and didn't wait for an answer. "You and your brother are to stay with the horses until I send someone to take your place."

"You get to tell us what to do, is that how it is?" Charles snapped.

"Father said we are to do whatever he asks of us," Philip said.

"You can if you want. I refuse to be dictated to by a provincial." Charles went to leave.

Fargo had had enough. Grabbing Charles by the shoulder, he slammed him against the wagon.

Bristling, Charles swore in French, let go of his rifle, and cocked his fist.

"I wouldn't," Philip warned.

Charles didn't heed.

Fargo ducked under a loping right. Taking a step back, he tossed his Henry to Philip and faced Charles just as the older brother delivered an uppercut. Slipping aside, Fargo slammed his right fist into Charles's gut and followed through with a left to the jaw.

Just like that, Charles's knees buckled and he fell against the wagon wheel and clutched it for support.

His head bobbed and he gazed groggily about him as if he didn't know where he was.

"Him and that temper of his," Philip said. He held out the Henry.

"Not yet," Fargo said.

Charles shook his head and muttered. His eyes cleared and he glared. "I will break you for that affront, American. Do you hear me?"

"I'm quaking in my boots," Fargo said.

With a curse, Charles heaved erect and came at him in a boxing stance. "I have had training, I'll have you know," he crowed. He flicked a cross, missed, and tried a low blow.

"You should get your money back," Fargo said, and drove his fist into Charles's chest below the sternum.

Charles cried out. He staggered and wheezed and a flush spread from his neck to his hair. He grabbed at the wheel again but missed and pitched to his hands and knees.

Philip said wearily, "I would feel sorry for him if he wasn't so stupid."

"I heard that, brother," Charles sputtered. His body shook and he glowered at Fargo with twice as much hate, if that was possible. "You have been lucky so far in besting me."

"Luck has nothing to do with it," Philip said. "He is quicker than you and stronger than you. He doesn't need luck."

Yells rose at the river. Louis and Henriette and the others were hastening over, Henriette shouting her oldest's name over and over.

"Here comes Mommy to the rescue," Fargo said.

Charles became a beet. He slowly rose and swiped at dirt and grass on his pants and his shirt.

"Are you done?" Fargo demanded.

"*Oui*," Charles said. "For now."

"Not good enough," Fargo said, and punched him below the belt.

Falling against the wagon, Charles clutched himself and groaned.

"Monsieur Fargo," Philip chided, "that was not very sportsmanlike."

Fargo moved in close to Charles. "It's over, for good. Or I'll do it again."

"You damned lout," Charles fumed. "How dare you treat me like this?" He started to raise a fist but thought better of it.

All at once the rest of the family was there.

Henriette flew to Charles and threw her arms around him. "You struck him!" she said to Fargo. "You hurt my son."

The twins, still wet-eyed from weeping at the funeral, gave Fargo withering stares.

Louis looked at Fargo and made clucking sounds of disapproval. "What went on here?"

"Charles provoked him, Father," Philip said.

Breaking free of his mother, Charles shook a fist at his brother. "*I* provoked *him*? He struck first, or have you forgotten?"

"Only because you missed," Philip said.

Charles might have torn into him had Louis not stepped between them.

"That will be quite enough. We have lost your aunt to a wild beast and are besieged by savages and you two behave in this childish manner?"

"What did I do?" Philip said.

Henriette was trembling with fury. "How can you blame our son? It's not their conduct, it's *his*," she said, and she jabbed a finger at Fargo. "You never should have hired this upstart."

"We needed a scout, my dear," Louis said. "I know you argued against it. You thought we could manage on our own. By now you should realize that's not true."

"What has he done that we couldn't do on our own? We can follow the river the same as him. We could find buffalo if we looked long enough."

"Dear, there are more important matters at the moment," Louis said.

Fargo wanted to take the whole bunch of them and shake them until their teeth rattled. "Are you through with the family squabble?"

"I beg your pardon?" Louis said.

Fargo moved to the end of the wagon and indicated the red stain. "They're out there, right now. Any moment they can put an arrow into any one of us."

Louis came over and gasped. "The poor man who was taken!"

He glanced at his wife. "We must put our differences aside for our mutual protection."

Charles bleated in disgust. "The red men will not dare attack us openly in broad daylight with all the guns we have."

As if to prove him wrong, an arrow whizzed out of the undergrowth and embedded itself in Bertrand.

19

It struck the Frenchman in the chest with a loud fleshy *thwuck*. For a few moments everyone was rooted in horror. Then one of the twins screamed, and panic erupted. Men fired blindly at the vegetation. Henriette threw her arms over Blanche and Jeanne and propelled them toward the big tent. Charles and Claude Dupree went, too, one on either side to protect them. The count bellowed to try and restore order.

Fargo was in a crouch at the end of the wagon, the Henry in his hands. He had a good idea where the arrow came from, but the warrior had gone to ground. "Get down!" he roared at the others, but only a few heard him and listened.

The shooting finally stopped.

Bertrand lay on his back, his legs bent, his fingers splayed at the sky, frozen by death.

Louis, staying low to the ground, scrambled to Fargo's side. "What do we do? Go into the woods after them?"

"That's just what they want," Fargo said. "So they can pick more of you off."

"Then what are we to do?" Louis asked as Philip scuttled over.

"Post two men at the tents, three men around the horses, the rest along the perimeter," Fargo instructed. "They're to stay low and keep their eyes peeled until I get back."

"Where are you going?"

Fargo nodded at the forest.

"Alone?" The count looked at his youngest and they both looked worried.

"Alone?" Philip repeated. "When there are ten of the savages?"

"I won't be long," Fargo said.

"I urge you not to," Louis said. "If we lose you, we are in dire straits."

"You won't lose me."

"Do not make a promise you might not be able to keep," Louis said. "But very well. We will do as you say."

Plainly unhappy, he went to give the orders to his men.

Philip said, "I insist on going with you, Monsieur Fargo."

"Like hell you will." Fargo saw a thicket move slightly.

"It is better there are two of us," Philip insisted. "I can watch your back and you can watch mine."

"No," Fargo said flatly. He couldn't do what he had to and look out for the boy, as well. To lessen the sting he put his hand on Philip's shoulder and said, "I need someone here I can trust not to lose his head."

"Me, monsieur?" Philip said.

"Your brother has that temper of his and Claude is a jackass."

"My father will keep them in line."

"It's best he has you to back him," Fargo said. He saw that men were moving toward the string and the tent and others were spreading out.

Flattening, Fargo said so only Philip would hear, "If I'm not back in an hour, I never will be." With that he crawled across a few feet of open space into the forest.

Fargo had dealt with Comanches before. The war party would harass the French, killing ever so often to instill fear. Unable to sleep, jumping at shadows, the whites would be easy prey when the Comanches attacked in force. There was only one way to prevent that from happening. He must instill fear in *them*.

As silently as a stalking cougar, Fargo crawled to a log and from there to a boulder and from there to a small spruce. He was working his way to the other side of the thicket he had seen move.

An oak with a wide trunk was his next cover. From behind it he spied a pair of legs and moccasins poking out of the thicket.

Now came the hard part. He must make no noise at all. He inched forward, moving an arm and a leg and then the other arm and the other leg. He was halfway there when his belt buckle snagged. There was the muffled crunch of a twig, and he froze. He didn't think the warrior had heard, but Comanches had sharp ears. Every nerve tingling, he waited. When the legs stayed still, he crept closer.

The warrior had crawled partway into the thicket and was staring out at the camp. He appeared to be interested in the horses.

Hankered to steal them, Fargo reckoned. Comanches were some of the best horsemen anywhere and valued their warhorses more than their wives.

He was only a few feet from the moccasins. Stopping, he quietly set the Henry down. He slid his right leg up and dipped his fingers into his boot. His fingers molded to the hilt of the Arkansas toothpick.

The warrior raised his head.

Fargo turned to stone, thinking the Comanche had heard him, or somehow sensed him. But no. Henriette had come out of the tent and was arguing with Louis. To a Comanche it was unthinkable, a woman berating a man the way the countess was berating the count.

The warrior seemed fascinated.

Fargo rose onto his elbows and knees. He tensed, dug the toes of his boots into the dirt, and exploded into motion. A bound brought him down on the warrior's back. Instantly, the Comanche attempted to turn.

Fargo thrust the toothpick to the hilt in the side of the warrior's neck. One stab was all it took. The man stiffened and his mouth gaped, but he didn't cry out. He gave a shudder and collapsed.

Fargo pulled the blade out. Some blood sprayed but not nearly as much as if he had pulled the knife out while the heart was still beating. He wiped the steel clean on the warrior's buckskins and slid off.

Odds were the Comanches had the clearing surrounded. Since there were only ten, they must be ranged twenty to thirty yards apart. He crawled on, alert for the next. As it was, he almost missed him. He was threading through cottonwoods when from off to his left came the crackle of a dry leaf. Stopping, he pressed as flat as he could and searched for the cause.

A warrior was crouched beside a tree, his attention fixed on the whites. He held a bow with an arrow notched to the string.

Twisting, Fargo left the Henry there. He had the toothpick in his right hand.

The Comanche rose partway as if to see better. He brought the bow up but after a bit lowered it.

Fargo stayed still until the warrior squatted back down. He

mustn't let the man hear him. Comanches were trained in the use of the bow from an early age. A skilled warrior could let six or seven arrows fly in a minute's time. If he gave the warrior any forewarning, he was in trouble.

Fortunately, the warrior was intent on the whites to the exclusion of all else.

As eager as the man appeared to be to use his bow, Fargo wondered if this was the one who slew Bertrand. Scarcely breathing, he edged nearer. Ten feet separated them. Then six. Then three. He eased into a crouch, coiled his legs, and was set to spring when the unforeseen occurred.

The warrior turned to go. He took a step, and saw him.

Fargo leaped. He lanced the toothpick at the same split second that the warrior jerked the bow up. His blade glanced off the bow. Shifting, he drove the knife at the warrior's belly, but the Comanche struck his wrist, deflecting his arm.

Unexpectedly, the warrior let go of the bow and took a step back. His hand streaked to his hip, and an antler-handled knife flashed in the sunlight.

This was the last thing Fargo needed. He sought to end it quickly by cutting at the warrior's throat.

The Comanche skipped aside and with almost feline speed and grace, pivoted and came at him in a burst of raw ferocity.

Suddenly Fargo was fighting for his life. The warrior was skilled, damn skilled, and it took every iota of Fargo's ability to counter and parry and ward off the death the Comanche was trying so determinedly to deal. He retreated under the onslaught of the warrior's weaving blade, and the Comanche, sensing weakness, pressed harder.

Fargo was all too aware that other warriors might rush to this one's aid at any moment. He dodged an attempt to disembowel him. He ducked a thrust at his face. He feinted left and went right, but the warrior sprang out of reach.

Fargo went after him. He slashed. He speared the toothpick's tip at the warrior's gut and met empty air. The Comanche was ungodly quick. Fargo feinted left again and instead of stabbing right he feinted left and went left.

The warrior grunted as the double-edged steel sliced into him to the hilt. His back arched, and he raised his face to the canopy and the sky.

Fargo thought the Comanche was going to cry out and he went to clamp his hand over the man's mouth. But the warrior caved without uttering a sound. A few twitches and it was over.

Fargo let out a breath. Once more he wiped the toothpick clean. Retrieving the Henry, he pondered his next move. To try to kill three was pushing his luck, and as Charles had reminded him, no one's luck held forever.

With infinite care, Fargo worked his way to the clearing. A nervous sentry snapped a rifle up and then saw it was him and said something in French.

A pall of grim expectancy hung over the camp. Hardly anyone spoke. A fire had been stoked and a female servant was tending a teapot.

Bertrand's body had been placed in a wagon bed until it was safe to bury him.

The count was in front of the big tent, seated on a cot. His sons were with him, but the women, and Claude, were inside. "You are back safely!" he said with genuine relief.

"It was foolhardy of you to go off like that," Charles said. "What purpose did it serve?"

"We'll find out soon enough." Fargo nodded at the servant. "She shouldn't be out here."

"Surely they wouldn't harm a woman?" Louis said. "Have they no honor?"

"Whites are their enemies, female or no."

"They are despicable, these savages," Charles sneered. "Cowards who refuse to face us man to man."

Fargo sighed. "The Comanches are a lot of things, but yellow isn't one of them."

"How can you say that after how they killed Bertrand?" Charles demanded.

"To their way of thinking, it's smart."

"I would like to see them try that again now that we are ready for them," Charles said.

Incredibly, an arrow streaked out of the woods—at his father.

20

Fargo reacted without thinking. He threw himself at Louis, who squawked as he was slammed off the cot to the ground.

Above them there was the buzz of the shaft and then a scream from inside the tent.

"Mon père!" Philip yelled.

Charles spun and fired at the forest, shouting in French. To a man, those in the clearing sent a fusillade into the woods.

Fargo doubted that they hit anything, but it might make the Comanches hunt cover. Rising, he slipped a hand under the count's arm and assisted him to his feet.

"Why did you do that, monsieur?" Louis asked, flustered.

"Papa," Philip said, and pointed at a hole in the tent. *"Il était une fleche."*

"The women!" Louis cried, and darted inside, his son on his heels.

Fargo trailed after them. He heard groaning and sobs.

Henriette and the twins and several servants were gathered around a maid. She was writhing in torment with her teeth grit.

The arrow had caught her above her right hip. The tip had gone clean through and over six inches jutted out. Blood trickled from both wounds.

Everyone was talking at once, in French. Henriette was trying to get the maid to lie still, but she wouldn't stop thrashing.

Louis bent to help her and was pushed away.

The maid let out another sob.

"Oh, hell," Fargo said, and shouldered through. Grabbing Henriette by the arm, he hauled her erect and shoved. "Hot water and bandages," he said, "as quick as you can."

"How dare you lay a hand on me!"

"I need those bandages pronto." Fargo dipped to one knee,

seized hold of the maid's shoulders, and pressed. "Enough, damn it. I can't get that out with you acting up."

Philip bent and addressed her in French, apparently translating. The maid stopped thrashing but broke into tears and lay quaking like an aspen leaf.

Fargo examined the arrow. It had missed the bone, and her vitals, and she wasn't bleeding excessively. He motioned at Philip.

"*Oui*, monsieur?"

"Tell her I'm going to take the arrow out. Tell her it will hurt like hell and for her to lie as still as she can."

Philip relayed his instructions, then asked, in English, "Is there anything I can do?"

"Hold her hand."

Charles was hovering behind them. "Have one of the other servants do it. We shouldn't be familiar with the hired help."

Fargo looked at him.

"What?" Charles said.

Philip clasped the young woman's hand and spoke soothingly. She smiled, and grew calmer.

"Thatta boy," Fargo encouraged him. He gripped the arrow near the barbed tip with one hand, and with his other grabbed hold where it had entered her body. "Tell her in advance that I'm sorry."

"For what, monsieur?" Philip translated her reply.

"This," Fargo said, and exerting all his strength, he broke the tip off.

The maid came up off the ground with her body bent. She shuddered, and mewed, then collapsed, mumbling, with sweat caking her face and neck.

"Tell her this next might make her feel sick," Fargo said. "Say the best thing for her to do is close her eyes and stay calm."

"Monsieur?"

"Just tell her." Fargo shifted and clamped both hands on the shaft above the feathers.

"Oh my," Philip said, divining his purpose. "I don't know if I can watch. I am already queasy."

"If we don't take it right out, she might become infected," Fargo observed. He didn't add that severe infections were nearly always fatal.

"I understand. She says that she is ready whenever you are."

Fargo smiled and the maid smiled at him and some of the tension went out of her. The slower he went, the worse she would feel, so he yanked on the arrow with all his might. Sometimes they came right out. Sometimes they didn't. Slick with blood and gore, this one slid free, as easy as could be.

The maid's eyelids fluttered but she didn't pass out.

Fargo held the dripping arrow where she could see it, then gave it to Philip.

"What should I do with this, monsieur?"

"Shove it up your brother's ass."

"I heard that," Charles said. "I am standing right here."

"I reckon I mistook you for a pile of elk shit," Fargo said.

"What have I done that you talk to me like that?" Charles demanded.

"Ask the hired help."

The twins appeared, carrying clean towels.

"Here you are," one said.

"Mother will bring hot water in another minute," said the other.

Fargo gently pressed cloths to both wounds. The maid would have scars but she'd live.

"Do you think the tip was poisoned?" Philip asked, patting her hand.

Fargo picked up the tip and sniffed the barbed point. He shook his head.

"*Dieu merci,*" Philip breathed. "She is a sweet girl, this one. Always polite and considerate."

Presently Henriette returned, followed by a servant carrying a large bowl brimming with hot water. "Let me," she said, and without waiting for Fargo to move, she squatted, took a cloth, and began tending to the maid's wounds herself.

Fargo went out.

Claude Dupree was by the wagons, pacing. Half a dozen others were with him, all peering anxiously into the woods.

Thinking they had spotted a Comanche, Fargo ran over. "What did you see?"

"Nothing," Claude said. "Three of our men went after the savage who nearly killed the count. We are waiting for them to return."

"They went out on their own?"

"*Non.* I sent them."

"No one was to go anywhere without my say-so," Fargo reminded him.

"You are not the only one who can give orders," Claude said. "As the *comte*'s brother-in-law, I have some small authority."

It took every ounce of self-control Fargo had not to pistol-whip him. "How long have they been gone?"

"Since shortly after you went into the tent. They should have been back. I don't understand it. We haven't heard any shots or outcries."

"I'll go find them," Fargo said, and moved between the wagons. "Keep everyone here." He glanced at Claude. "And this time you'd better damn well listen."

Gliding into the trees, Fargo crouched. The three Frenchmen had walked so close together, out of fear, he guessed, that they'd left a plain trail of bent grass and other sign. He went on, slowly. To be rash was to be dead.

The first body was only a stone's throw from the clearing. Judging by the size of the hole, an arrow had transfixed the man's throat from front to back. It had been yanked out. Indians never left arrows behind if they could help it; too much work went into making them. The man's nose had been chopped off and an ear was missing.

From the way the victim was lying, Fargo reckoned that he'd been facing the clearing when he was slain, which suggested he was on his way back.

Fargo continued on. Deathly silence had fallen. Not so much as the chirp of a bird was to be heard.

The second body was farther out. This one's throat had been slit from ear to ear and the face mutilated beyond recognition.

Both men had been stripped of their weapons. Neither had been scalped even though both had a full head of hair.

Fargo thought he heard a footstep and dropped flat.

When minutes went by and the woods stayed quiet, he cautiously rose. He crept a considerable distance and found where a struggle had taken place.

As he reconstructed it, all three Frenchmen had made it this far. They were jumped, and two turned and fled. The Comanches gave chase, caught one and slit his throat, went after the other and shot him with an arrow.

As for the third man, drag marks led to where horses had been tied. All the horses—and the Comanches—were gone. They'd taken the third Frenchman with them.

"Damn," Fargo said. Standing, he hurried to the clearing. He ran to the ovaro and was in the saddle before Claude caught up to him.

"Wait, monsieur! Where are you off to? What happened to the three men I sent out?"

"Two are dead, you idiot."

"No."

"The third was taken captive. He'll be tortured unless I can save him."

"I am going with you."

"Over my dead body." Fargo reined around and resorted to his spurs. How long the captive lived depended on whether the war party intended to take him back to their village or they were only going far enough away that his screams wouldn't be heard.

Fargo was tired and hungry. The day was taking its toll. If he had his druthers he wouldn't tangle with eight Comanches, but he was the captive's only hope.

The war party had headed northwest. They weren't in any hurry. They must figure the whites wouldn't come after them.

For over a mile the plain was mostly flat. In a while grassy knolls broke the monotony.

Beyond, like so many giant tombstones, isolated bluffs dotted the prairie.

Soon the sun brushed the horizon.

Fargo pushed the ovaro. Unless he overtook them before dark, he would have to wait until morning. By then the captive would be dead.

If he had any sense, Fargo told himself, he'd turn back. Here he was, risking his hide for a man he didn't know.

Then he heard the scream.

21

Twilight was falling.

Fargo had left the ovaro in a wash and was cat-footing along the base of a flat-topped bluff. Plenty of boulders provided cover.

The cries of agony had been going on for almost ten minutes: screams, shrieks, gabbles of torment from a mind teetering on the edge.

Fargo peered around a boulder, and froze. He had found the Comanches.

A small fire danced red and orange. A dead doe lay near it. None of the warriors were interested in eating, though. They were standing around the captive.

The man had been stripped naked and staked out on his back. He was helpless to prevent what they were doing to him.

They'd already taken his scalp. Indians did that sometimes, took the hair when their enemy was alive. They'd cut off his ears, too. His lips had been peeled away and lay on his chest. He was blubbering and sniffling, and that amused them.

On his belly, Fargo snaked closer. Red puddles drew his attention to the Frenchman's hands; all the victim's fingers had been chopped off and left in small piles.

A warrior was straddling him, and grinning. Only when the warrior shifted did Fargo see that they had also cut off something else, lower down.

Bile rose in Fargo's gorge. He swallowed it and came to the next boulder and stopped. He was about twenty yards out. It would have to do. The warriors had a few rifles—those taken from the men they'd killed—as well as bows.

The Frenchman began to beg. He pleaded. He wept.

It amused the Comanches even more.

Fargo took aim. He noticed small reddish white objects lying near the man's head. They were teeth, smeared in blood.

The warrior on the Frenchman's chest poked him with a knife and the man wept harder.

The Comanches laughed.

The warrior stood and moved aside and another stepped up and jabbed the Frenchman in the belly with a lance. Not deep, but enough that blood welled and the Frenchman dithered like a lunatic.

Fargo held his breath to steady the Henry and curled his finger around the trigger. "I'm sorry," he said softly, and fired.

The slug struck just above the ear and exploded out the other side of the Frenchman's cranium in a spectacular spray of flesh and bone.

For a few moments the Comanches were riveted in surprise. Then one whooped and they all turned in the direction of the shot.

Fargo was up and running. Some would come after him on foot. He wasn't worried about them. He was worried about the warriors who had the presence of mind to run to their horses.

An arrow whizzed out of the darkening sky and shattered on a boulder wide to his left.

A rifle boomed and the lead spanged off a boulder to his right.

Fargo wished it was darker. In the dark he could lose them. Maybe fifteen minutes of light was left. Enough for them to catch him and kill him. He glanced back. Five or six were in pursuit on foot. Farther back, two on horseback were just starting out after him. Both had bows.

Fargo was going as fast as he could. A misstep would prove fatal. He avoided a rock, vaulted a low boulder. Hugging the shadow at the base of the bluff, he flew for his life.

The Comanches yipped and howled. It was said that a Comanche war whoop could curdle a soul with fear.

Legs pumping, boots slapping the earth, Fargo ran and ran.

Another arrow sought his life.

Another shot clipped slivers from stone.

After that the Comanches didn't waste any more shafts or bullets. They were grim two-legged wolves intent on their prey.

Fargo swept around a bend. The wash and the ovaro were up ahead.

Behind him, hooves clattered.

The two on horseback had passed the rest on foot. They were side by side, whooping ferociously.

Fargo was almost to the wash. It was now or never. Stopping, he whirled and wedged the Henry to his shoulder. He fired at the warrior on the right, jacked the lever to feed a new cartridge into the chamber, and fired at the warrior on the left. In a short spring he was in the wash. He shoved the Henry in the scabbard and swung onto the saddle. A wrench on the reins, twin prods of his spurs, and he was away.

The Comanches were shrieking in outrage and bloodlust.

Fargo followed the wash for more than a hundred yards. Low over the saddle horn, he rode up and out and galloped into the night.

The wind on his face, the cool night air, felt wonderful.

When he had gone a mile, he was fairly certain the Comanches weren't coming after him.

Fargo slowed and patted the ovaro. Once again the stallion had saved his hash. Some folks wondered why he was so fond of it. A good horse, like a good dog, was more than an animal. It was a friend.

The count's party had built their fires much too big. They probably thought they had to. The more light, the more secure they felt. Little did they realize it was a beacon.

Fargo didn't expect the Comanches to return. They'd lost four of their own, and that was enough. Despite what a lot of Easterners thought, Indians weren't stupid. They didn't throw their lives away.

Bone tired, Fargo growled a curt reply when a sentry challenged him. He rode into the circle and dismounted and was promptly surrounded.

"Where have you been?" Louis asked. "I have been worried sick."

Fargo put a hand on his shoulder. "You'd do to ride the river with, count."

"Monsieur?"

Henriette had her hands on her hips and disdain on her face. "My husband asked where you have been. We brought the two bodies from the forest while you were gone and buried them. But where is Armand, the third man who went missing?"

"Dead." Fargo opened his saddlebags and took out his tin cup. He needed coffee, badly.

"The savages killed him?" Louis asked.

"I did." Fargo shouldered through them and over to a fire. Squatting, he filled his cup with steaming hot coffee and gratefully sipped.

They followed, regarding him with a mix of consternation and wrath.

"Monsieur Fargo," Louis said. "Surely I did not hear you right. *You* killed Armand?"

"Blew his brains out," Fargo said, and savored another sip.

Charles balled his fists and took a step. "What sort of animal are you, American?"

"*Oui,*" Claude Dupree said. "What possible reason could you have? Explain it to us or by God I will thrash you."

"No," Fargo said. "You won't."

"Monsieur Fargo, please," the count said.

Fargo told them. He left nothing out. He gave them every grim and horrible detail: the scalp, the lips, everything. When he was done their faces were pale and some were slick with sweat and more than a few Adam's apples bobbed.

"*Oui.* Now I understand," Louis said softly. "You shot him to put him out of his misery."

"With all due respect, *Comte,*" Claude said, "this incompetent should have shot the savages and brought poor Armand back."

"To what end?" Louis retorted. "Would you want to live if they did to you what they did to him?"

"Well, I—" Claude began.

The count stopped him with a sharp gesture. "No, Claude, you would not. Monsieur Fargo did the right thing and I will not hear criticism to the contrary."

"Of course you won't," Henriette said bitterly.

"My dear?"

"You forgive him too readily, husband. You forget that this precious scout of yours is little better than the savages who attacked us."

"Not true," the count said. "He has proven to be as civilized as any of us."

"Oh, please," Henriette said, and launched into French. They argued, until finally she hissed and turned and marched to the big tent. The twins went with her.

"My apologies," Louis said to Fargo. "It is the strain of losing her sister."

Fargo thought it was the fact that Henriette was a bitch, but for the count's sake he didn't say anything.

"Father," Charles said, "I propose we head back to Corpus Christi without delay."

"After all the money and time I've invested?"

"What are they compared to Mother's life? And the lives of Blanche and Jeanne? We have already lost Odette. Would you lose them, as well?"

"I agree," Claude said. "If it were our own lives I would say push on. But we have the women to think of."

Louis turned to his youngest. "And what do you say, my son?"

Philip hesitated. "I am sorry, Father. I must side with Charles and Claude."

"You, as well?" Louis said, sounding stricken.

"Monsieur Fargo was right," Philip said. "He warned us of the perils, but we wouldn't listen. Now five of our number are dead and the expedition has barely begun. Who can say how many more we will lose if we continue?"

Louis's shoulders sagged. "I must think awhile. Perhaps you are right. Were anything to happen to your mother or your sisters, I would never forgive myself."

He walked off, his head bowed.

"I pray to God he comes to his sense," Charles said. "I have had enough of this barbaric country."

Claude said something in French.

Looking down at Fargo, Charles sneered. "Yes. My father is not the only one at fault."

The pair moved toward the tent.

"I am sorry, monsieur," Philip said, "for how poorly my family treats you."

Fargo thought of Jeanne's firm breasts and of her gushing with her legs wrapped around him, and he hid a smile behind his cup. "Not all of you."

"Of more immediate concern are the Comanches. You know them better than we do. Do you think they will attack us again?"

"It's unlikely."

"Then if Father agrees to turn back," Philip said happily, "the worst is over."

"I wouldn't count on it," Fargo said.

22

It was the middle of the night when the ovaro nickered.

Fargo was deep in sleep. He'd finally crawled under his blankets about midnight and been so tired, he drifted off the moment he closed his eyes. Now he struggled to rouse, aware that the stallion never whinnied like that without cause. He was about to succumb to more slumber when the ovaro nickered a second time and stomped a hoof.

Suddenly Fargo was wide awake. He was on his side, his back to the fire.

All was still.

A sentry sat at one of the fires, dozing. Here and there the bundled forms of sleepers dotted the clearing.

Pretending to mutter, Fargo rolled onto his back. He cracked his eyelids and looked out of the corners of his eyes.

Two sentries were talking by the wagons.

Fargo didn't understand it. No one else was about and the woods were quiet. He was beginning to think that for once the ovaro had acted up for no reason when something moved along the tree line past the tents. A Comanche, he reckoned, and under his blanket he slid his hand to his Colt.

The figure paused and glanced at the guards. In the flickering firelight, Fargo made out a flowing garment, and a hood.

It was a woman. But whether it was Henriette or one of the twins, he couldn't say. Whoever she was, when she was sure the sentries weren't looking, she darted around the tent and was inside before Fargo could get a good look. He was about to sit up when a second figure appeared.

This one was a man. He was hunched over and wearing some sort of cloak and floppy hat. He came along the tree line as the woman had done, paused as she had done, and slipped inside.

Fargo threw his blankets off and stood. He went to the tent and gripped the flap, but it wouldn't open. The man had tied it shut. He debated yelling to wake the count, but what purpose would it serve? He had no idea what the man and woman had been up to. And whoever the two were, they'd undoubtedly deny skulking around.

Puzzled, Fargo returned to his blankets. He sat and was pulling the top blanket up when he noticed that the guard dozing by the fire had slumped forward and his head was practically in the flames.

"What the hell?" Getting back up, Fargo went over. "Wake up, lunkhead. You're about to catch on fire."

The sentry didn't move.

"Didn't you hear me?" Fargo nudged him.

The man slowly keeled onto his side. His eyes were wide in death. Traces of a white froth rimmed his lips and had dried on his chin.

"Son of a bitch," Fargo said, and hunkered. He saw the dart right away; it was in the man's neck, above the collar.

Fargo didn't know what to make of it. Why kill a sentry? Unless whoever did it was afraid the sentry would see them doing something they shouldn't, such as leaving the tent in the middle of the night.

This time he didn't hesitate. He strode to the tent and shook the flap and hollered. Around and behind him, men sat up and called out to one another.

A light glowed in the tent. Then another. Voices and footfalls came close and the flap opened.

"What is the meaning of this?" Louis asked. He was in his nightshirt and his hair stuck up like spikes. "Why have you woken us at this uncivilized hour?"

"See for yourself." Crooking a finger, Fargo led the count to the fire.

Others converged. Excited whispers broke out as the murder dawned.

"Yet another one," Louis said sorrowfully. "At this rate I will not have enough men to ward off another Indian attack."

The count's family was unusually quiet. Henriette and the twins were bundled in robes. Philip and Charles were in nightshirts.

Claude emerged from his tent wearing a silk nightshirt with a fur collar.

"In all the excitement with the savages," Philip said, "I forgot about the killer with the blowgun."

"I didn't," Fargo said.

"Nor have I," Henriette said. "It is yet another reason I want to turn back."

"Pick a burial detail," Louis said to Claude. "We will bury him next to Odette."

"You will do no such thing," Henriette quickly said. "I do not want a commoner next to my sister. We must observe the proprieties. Bury him with the men the savages killed."

"Odette is past caring."

"I'm not," Henriette said. She plucked at the arms of Blanche and Jeanne. "You should not see this. Get back to bed."

"*Que vous le souhaitez, ma mère,*" one of them said.

Louis said, "We must double the sentries. Do you agree, Monsieur Fargo?"

Fargo nodded. "Post them at the tents. One in front and another in back."

"The tents?" Louis said.

Henriette stopped and looked back. "What was that? Why do we need guards to watch over us?"

"You don't," Fargo said.

"Then why . . ." Henriette stopped. "Oh. *Je voix.* You don't want to protect us. You believe the killer is one of us." She glared at the count. "What about this, Louis? Are we to be treated as if we are prisoners in our own camp?"

"It seems a prudent precaution, my dear."

"I, for one, won't stand for it," Claude said.

"You sure as hell will," Fargo said, and placed his hand on his Colt.

"Is that a threat, monsieur?"

Fargo smiled. "It sure as hell is."

They filed into the tent, arguing.

By the next morning the count had made his decision. Louis called them all together shortly after the sun claimed the sky. His family, the servants, the drivers, everyone. He addressed them in French, and Philip, standing at his side, translated.

"We are returning to Corpus Christi. I do this with the utmost reluctance. For years I looked forward to a grand adventure in the American West, and now my dream has been shattered. But with all the deaths, and the constant threat of the Comanches, I must put aside my personal feelings and do what is best for the common good."

"*Dieu merci,*" Henriette said.

Charles said, "*L'est temps, mon père.*"

"We will enjoy a leisurely breakfast," Louis said, "and then pack and get under way. I hope none of you will consider this cowardice on my part. I assure you that were it entirely up to me I would not go back. My family, however, is united in their opposition."

"Even me," Philip whispered to Fargo.

"So let us cast off our worries and be confident in a very few days we will be safe and sound, as the Americans say."

Fargo passed on breakfast. He wasn't hungry. He did have a cup of coffee. Then, after saddling the ovaro, he informed the count that he would scout around while everyone got ready to head out.

Philip offered to go along, but Fargo told him no.

The sky was clear, the air crisp, the woods alive with animal life. It was the wilds at its best, picturesque and peaceful, and anyone else might have been lulled into a false feeling that all was well. Not Fargo. He knew the treachery of the wilderness, how it could be serene one minute and the next a grizzly would come crashing out of the brush or hostiles would appear out of nowhere.

Fargo made for the Nueces. He rode along the bank for a while but saw no sign that the Comanches had crossed recently or watered their mounts. He searched the woods for a quarter of a mile in both directions and again didn't find cause to worry.

The camp bustled with activity when he rejoined them. The tents were being taken down, the provisions repacked, the teams hitched to the wagons.

Fargo indulged in more coffee. He was on his second cup when Louis came over.

Today the count wore a purple coat, of all things, and a white shirt with ruffles. His coat was open and under it a gold belt buckle gleamed. His pants were a European style that tapered at the ankles and his shoes had high heels and shiny brass buttons. "A word, if you please."

Fargo grunted.

"First, I want to assure you that even though I have cut my trip shot, you will receive the full five thousand."

"I'm obliged."

"Second, I'd like to talk about this dart business." Louis looked around as if to be sure no one could hear him.

"All morning I have been thinking about that sentry and why he was murdered. There are only two explanations."

"I'm all ears," Fargo said.

"Either he was part of the plot with the killer and the killer silenced him to keep him from telling anyone—"

"I don't think so," Fargo broke in.

"—or he was shot with a dart because he saw something he shouldn't."

Fargo remembered the two people who had snuck into the big tent. "That was my guess."

"Regardless," Louis continued, "the danger is far from over. Whoever is behind this might strike again. And the devil of it is, we have no idea why."

"You can't think of any of them who might be up to no good?" Fargo asked bluntly.

"My own family?" Louis shook his head. "You've seen how they are. Yes, we squabble, as families often do, but we are devoted to each other. They all know that so long as I live I will provide for them handsomely, and when I die, they will each receive an inheritance that will have them set for life."

Fargo had a notion that sent a tingle down his spine. It was the one thing that made sense of the whole mess. "Tell me," he said, "do you French gamble much?"

"Gamble, monsieur? As in cards and dice? *Oui*. We are inveterate gamblers. Have you never heard of roulette? It was invented in France. And some say blackjack, as well."

"You don't say."

"I gambled some when I was younger," Louis related. "Before I was married, of course."

"Of course," Fargo said.

"Even women gamble in France. It is especially popular among the aristocracy."

"You don't say," Fargo said again.

"Henriette has never gambled, to my knowledge. She thinks it a frivolous waste. Neither did Odette. It bores Philip. But I think Charles gambles now and again."

"What about Claude?"

"I have never heard him mention spending any time at the tables," Louis said. "Why all these questions? What does it have to do with the killer with the blowgun?"

"Time will tell," Fargo said.

23

They had covered five miles when a couple of spokes on a wheel broke.

It would take half an hour to take the wheel off and replace them, so the count had stools set out for his family in the shade of trees at the prairie's edge.

Everyone was in fine spirits. They felt that the worst was over.

Fargo was scanning the horizon for sign of the Comanches when the driver of the wagon with the busted wheel came over. A Texan, the man had been hired in Corpus Christi.

"Need a word," the man said. "My handle is Walker. Ira Walker."

Fargo hadn't talked to the drivers much. They tended to stick to themselves and he was always busy with the count or off scouting. "What's on your mind?"

"These." Walker held out the four halves of the broken spokes.

Fargo examined them. The ends where the spokes had broken showed evidence of having been sawed partway through. "Son of a bitch."

"I reckoned as how you'd want to know," Walker said, and took out a plug and bit off a chaw.

"When?" Fargo wondered.

"It had to be last night," Walker said. "They were pretty clever about it. They sawed so the spokes held up awhile." He scratched his chin. "The thing I can't savvy is why. What do they get out of it other than delayin' us?"

"Keep this to yourself."

"Whatever you say, hoss." Walker stared toward the trees, and the family. "You ask me, these Frenchers are damned peculiar. It's not just that foreign lingo. I hear tell they eat snails."

"Anything else?"

"One of the other drivers thought he saw someone slinkin' about the camp last night. But he was half-asleep and didn't get a good look." Walker touched his hat brim and walked off.

Before they got under way, Fargo had the drivers go over their wagons from tongue to bed. The rest of the wheels were fine.

By late afternoon they had only covered five more miles.

A grassy area in a bend of the Nueces made an ideal campsite. While the rest were busy with the fires and the tents, Fargo left the ovaro and went hunting on foot. They could use fresh meat.

Deer were plentiful and it wasn't long before he spotted a doe and a fawn. He didn't shoot. The fawn was too young, and without her mother, she'd likely die.

On soundless soles he stalked the shadows until he saw a pool. Crouching, he waited. His patience was rewarded when an incautious buck came early to slake its thirst.

Fargo centered the Henry's sights and blew out the buck's brains.

He headed back for a packhorse. He'd tote the body for the cook to carve up and have juicy venison steak for supper.

The shot had silenced the wild things, but now they came back to life. A robin warbled and finches tweeted and somewhere a dove cooed.

Fargo rounded an oak and a feathered shaft missed him by inches and struck the trunk with a loud *thunk.* In reflex he dropped flat.

Fargo gauged where the arrow came from by the direction the feathers were pointing. He searched for the warrior but saw no one.

He'd reckoned the Comanches would leave them be, but apparently not.

Anxious to warn the others, Fargo made for the camp. For all he knew, the original war party had reached their village and come back with twice as many warriors. The count's people might be on the verge of being wiped out.

He went around a pine and slid over a log and still had a ways to go.

Off in the woods a twig cracked.

Fargo stopped. The arrow had come from his right. The twig that cracked was to his left. They had him surrounded.

He had a decision to make. Lie there and fight when they rushed him or try to reach the clearing. He didn't hesitate. He pushed up and ran.

An arrow missed by a whisker.

Fargo expected to hear war whoops and the crash of vegetation, but the only sounds were the pounding of his boots and the roar of his blood in his ears. To his surprise no more arrows were loosed. He reached the clearing in one piece.

"Comanches!" he bellowed. "Hunt cover, and hunt it quick!"

A mad scramble ensued. Men leaped up from fires, grabbed rifles, and ran to the wagons or crouched behind trees. Count Tristan and his family and servants dashed into their tents. Louis soon reappeared armed with his custom-made rifle, and with his sons at his side.

Fargo was by an oak, scouring the tangle of vegetation.

"Where are the red savages?" Louis asked as he dropped to a knee.

Fargo shook his head.

"I thought you said they wouldn't bother us again?" Charles asked angrily.

"Odds were," Fargo said.

"Yet here they are," Charles said. "If you ask me, monsieur, as a scout you are overrated."

"Please, brother," Philip said. "He does his best. There is no predicting with Indians."

"Naturally you defend him," Charles spat. "But I don't think as highly of him as you do, brother."

"Enough," Louis said. He turned to Fargo. "What do we do? Wait for them to attack? Or flee?"

"If we run they'd catch us out in the open," Fargo replied.

"Where we are most vulnerable. No, that would not be wise," Louis agreed.

"I'm going for a look-see," Fargo said. "No one else is to leave the camp." He repeated it. "No one."

"I give you my word that no one will."

With a nod, Fargo slipped into the woods. The ruckus had caused the creatures to go quiet. His skin prickling, he glided from shadow to shadow. Soon the sun would set and the Comanches could pick them off from the dark. He had to find out how many there were, and plan accordingly.

The minutes were eternities. A war whoop, and an arrow or lance, might cleave the air at any second.

Comanches were formidable fighters. Fargo wasn't about to underestimate them. That the one earlier had missed surprised him. Most seasoned warriors would have waited to let the arrow fly until they were absolutely sure.

Other than a few flies and a bee buzzing about, not so much as a leaf stirred.

Fargo was running out of time. Half the sun was gone.

He took a gamble and deliberately stepped on a fallen branch. At the crack, he dived flat. Nothing happened. He detected no movement, no whispers.

His puzzlement grew.

Presently he was near where he had been when the arrow missed. He cast about for sign and spied some, and stopped. The outline of a foot in a spot of bare earth put everything in a new light.

Fargo hunkered and traced the print with a finger. He swore, and stayed there awhile, recollecting all that had happened, and how from the very beginning he had been misled. The why of it still eluded him, but he would find that out soon enough.

Cradling the Henry, Fargo rose and walked back. He made no attempt to hide. He wasn't worried about the Comanches anymore.

Rifles were jerked up and lowered again when he came out of the shadows.

"Did you find them?" Louis anxiously inquired. "How serious is it?"

"Tell me something," Fargo said. "Those Comanches I shot at our last camp. What happened to them?"

Charles said, "We left them to rot. Why should we bury heathens?"

"And their weapons?" Fargo said. "One had a lance and the other had a bow."

"I don't recall," Louis said. "I imagine we left them lying in the woods."

"That is exactly what we did," Philip confirmed. "I remember seeing them there."

"Well, now," Fargo said.

"What is it, monsieur?" Louis said.

"I'll tell you what it is, Father," Charles said. "He spread a false alarm. There is no danger, is there? Or you would not be standing there so calmly."

"Anyone can make a mistake," Philip said.

"Especially him," Charles said in disgust, and stood. "I will inform Mother and the girls that they need not cower in fear."

"I have never known Mother to cower," Philip said.

Charles wheeled on a heel and stalked off.

"Is he right, monsieur?" Louis said. "Are we safe?"

"From the Comanches," Fargo said.

Most were elated by the news. A few looked at Fargo and grumbled. He took the ovaro and a packhorse and went to fetch the buck.

Philip offered to tag along and Fargo let him. "I must say," the younger man remarked as they were hoisting the buck over the packhorse, "I am sorry we have cut our visit so short. I've enjoyed your company very much."

"Not all of you have," Fargo said.

"Are you referring to Charles? He is that way toward everyone, even his own family."

"Has he ever killed anyone?"

"Charles?" Philip said, and laughed. "He has only ever killed a few animals, and then only to impress our father. He hates to hunt, hates to kill things. You wouldn't know it by how he behaves, but he has a very tender heart."

"You're right," Fargo said. "I don't believe it."

On the ride back it was so dark that a bowman would have to be an arm's length away to hit them. No one tried.

The prospect of fresh meat put most in good spirits. Half the buck was given to the men to roast over a fire. The rest the count turned over to the family cook to prepare a "proper meal" for his family.

They were seated on stools outside the big tent, the women included, when Fargo strolled over. He only had a few days in which to flush the culprits out, and now was as good a time as any to start.

"Monsieur Fargo, my good friend," the count greeted him warmly. "Come, take a stool and join us."

"No, thanks," Fargo said, and looked at each of them, even

the twins. "I just wanted to let you know that I've figured it out. I know who is out to kill me, and why."

Louis shot to his feet. "You do? You must tell us this instant."

"No."

"But why not?" Louis said in bewilderment. "I don't understand."

"It's between me and them," Fargo said, and he turned and walked off, fully aware he had just slapped the killers in the face and dared them to try again.

24

All the next day Fargo rode on a tightrope. He never turned his back to any of the family. When they stopped at midday, he sat with his back to a wagon wheel. He wasn't taking chances. Arrow or dart, it could be one or the other.

Along about three in the afternoon, they halted again, briefly. The temperature had climbed high into the nineties.

Fargo went to the rear of the column to check behind them for telltale signs of dust in the distance.

One of the twins rode over looking as fresh as a morning daisy, despite the sweltering heat. "We must talk, monsieur," she said sweetly.

"Jeanne or Blanche?" Fargo said. He still couldn't tell one from the other.

"Blanche," the twin said. "My sister is keeping my mother busy so we can have a few words."

"About?"

"About us making love," Blanche said. "It is my turn. I would very much like to have you tonight."

"You and your sister," Fargo said, and chuckled.

"We are not timid, Jeanne and I," Blanche said. "She has extolled you highly. I am eager to see if she told the truth."

Fargo thought about saying no. He couldn't afford to be distracted. Then he noticed the swell of her breasts and how the contours of her thighs showed through her dress. "When did you have in mind?"

"Tonight after everyone has fallen asleep. I will sneak out and come to you. *Est que tout va bien?* Is that all right?"

"Come naked," Fargo said.

Blanche laughed. "Would that I could. But were my parents

to catch me, oh *mon*, they would be scandalized. I would be sent to a nunnery."

"We wouldn't want that."

"I could not live without men," Blanche said. She raised her reins. "I hope you are all my sister claims. She likes to play games. Perhaps you are not as good as she pretends."

"You'll beg for more," Fargo said.

"That will be the day." Blanche laughed and rode up the line.

Fargo sighed and said to himself, "When the hell will I ever learn?"

Nightfall found them once again camped near the river. The horses had been watered, fires were burning, and sentries posted.

Fargo sat where he could see the flaps to both tents and whenever any of the family came out, he kept track of where they were at all times.

Unexpectedly, a pair of drivers came over. Their clothes were caked with dust, and both could use a wash.

One was Ira Walker. "This here is Garret." He introduced his companion. "Him and me are pards."

Garret nodded and spat a wad of tobacco. "Pleased to meet you, mister."

"We hear tell that somebody is out to plant you," Walker said.

"Who told you?"

"It's a rumor goin' around," Walker said.

"Is it true?" Garret asked.

"Appears to be," Fargo said.

They looked at each other.

"We'd like to offer to help," Walker said. "Anything we can do for you, we will."

"Oh?" Fargo said.

"Us Americans got to stick together against these blamed foreigners," Garret said.

"How do you know it's them trying to kill me?" Fargo asked. Come to think of it, he reflected, how did he know these two hadn't been hired for the job?

"Well, we don't, rightly," Walker admitted. "But who else would use a puny little dart to do their killin'?"

"Stupid foreigners can't do nothin' right," Garret said. He patted his six-gun. "They should use one of these."

"I'm grateful," Fargo said.

Walker waited as if expecting him to say more and when he didn't, he said, "So, do we lend you a hand or not? And if so, how?"

"You can watch my back."

"That's all?" Walker said, and grunted. "Hell, we can do that easy enough. You need more, say so."

Garret nodded. "I like to shoot foreigners as much as I like to shoot anybody."

"Have you ever shot anyone?" Fargo asked.

"Well, no. Not unless you count the Dutcher that time in that saloon. But I only shot him in the leg. I aimed higher but I was so damn drunk—"

Walker held up a hand. "I don't reckon Mr. Fargo cares to hear about your silly fight."

"Wasn't silly," Garret said. "That Dutcher stepped on my toe. I had cause to hit him. Then the blamed jackass went and pulled a knife on me."

"Anyway," Walker said, "we're here if you need us." He touched his hat brim and nudged his pard and they ambled away.

"Will wonders never cease?" Fargo said.

The big tent opened and out came Philip. He gazed about, spied Fargo, smiled, and hastened over.

"I bring you an invitation from my father to join us for supper."

"I'm fine here," Fargo said.

Philip frowned. "We only have a few nights left together. It would please me greatly. Much more so than Mother."

"Oh?"

"When Father mentioned asking you, she became angry and demanded he not do it. I imagine she will fume the entire meal."

"In that case," Fargo said, rising, "lead the way."

The family was seated as before at the long table. Crystal glasses and silver trays gleamed in the lantern light. Servants hovered, ready to respond to the slightest whim.

"Thank you for joining us," Louis said from the far end. "Have a seat."

Henriette sniffed as if the air had turned foul.

A servant went to pull Fargo's chair out for him and he shook his head, pulled it out himself, and sat.

"In civilized countries we don't mind being helped by those we pay to help us," Henriette said archly.

"In this country we pull down our own britches before we piss in the chamber pot," Fargo said.

Heads snapped up. One of the twins gasped. Claude Dupree turned red in the face and glowered. Charles tapped his soup spoon in irritation.

Henriette looked fit to explode. "Must you be so crude?"

"Everyone pisses," Fargo said.

"*Certainement,*" Henriette said. "But it is not a proper subject to bring up at the supper table."

"Enough," Louis said. "I did not invite Monsieur Fargo to join us just to hear more petty bickering."

"I would not call good manners petty," Henriette said.

"Nor I," Claude declared.

"Speaking of manners," Fargo said, "how do the French feel about killing folks?"

"Monsieur?" Louis said.

Fargo picked up his crystal glass and sipped some water to keep them waiting. "Two of you are out to kill me. In my country we don't call that good manners. We call it being a son of a bitch." He smiled at Henriette. "Or a bitch."

"Wait," Louis said. "Before you suspected one of us. Now you talk as if you are positive there are two?"

"Positive as positive can be," Fargo bluffed.

"Do you know who the two are?" Philip asked.

"I do," Fargo said without looking at any of them. They might detect the lie.

Louis leaned forward. "Tell us. I beg you. Who is out to murder you?"

"It's not you."

The count leaned even farther. "Yes, but who? *S'il vous plaît.* Don't keep us in suspense."

"That's just it," Fargo said. "I want to."

"Monsieur?" Louis said in confusion.

"I want them to know I know," Fargo said. "I want them to know that I'm on to them. An eye for an eye as it goes."

"What are you saying?" Charles asked.

Fargo gazed at each of them before replying, "That between here and Corpus Christi, two of you are going to die."

"Surely you can't mean us?" a twin said.

The corners of Henriette's mouth were twitching. "How crude. Yet I would expect no less from an uncultured bumpkin."

"At least us bumpkins aren't yellow."

"Monsieur?" Louis responded.

"Only a coward uses a blowgun," Fargo said. "Someone with no balls."

Henriette threw her silk napkin onto the table and pushed to her feet. "Enough. I will not sit here and listen to this vile language any longer."

"Sit back down," Louis said.

"You heard him, husband," Henriette said. "He does this deliberately, to bait us."

"Not them," Fargo said. "You."

Charles said, "Have a care, American. *Elle est ma mère.* She is my mother, and I will not stand to have her insulted."

"Nor I," Claude said.

Louis balled his fists. "Did none of you hear me? Since when am I not obeyed by my own family? I said *enough*!" He roared the last word and slammed the table. "You shame me with your conduct."

"Us?" Henriette said. "But we—"

Louis pounded the table so hard, his glass upended, spilling wine. A servant leaped to right the glass and he shoved the man away. "Why are you not in your chair?"

Blanching, Henriette sat.

"Comte Tristan, please—" Claude Dupree began.

Louis jabbed a finger at him. "One more word out of you and I will ban you from any contact with us, ever."

Claude looked stunned.

"What has gotten into you, husband?" Henriette asked anxiously.

Louis smiled. "As our guest might say, I have discovered I have balls. And I am with him in this. Whoever hired Alexandre Sifrein, whoever has made repeated attempts on Monsieur Fargo's life, must be held to account."

"But to treat us in this manner," Henriette said.

They bickered, but Fargo didn't listen. He was more interested in what was going on under the table.

The twin sitting next to him was rubbing her thigh against his.

25

It was like having a target painted on his back. Fargo didn't like it, but to draw the killers out he had to provoke them. Some might say that was loco. The best way to hunt ducks, though, was to set out a decoy. He couldn't help it if the only decoy he had was himself.

Along about midnight, Fargo sat with his back to his saddle and his Henry in his lap, facing the tents.

The family had turned in hours ago. So had the drivers and others. Only the four sentries were awake, and him.

Fargo yawned. He was tired. He'd love to lie down and drift off. But he had a gut feeling that something would happen.

His eyelids were growing heavy when the flap to the big tent parted. A head sheathed in blond hair poked out, and one of the twins dashed to the gap between the tents and looked at him.

Fargo was all interest. He checked that none of the sentries had noticed her.

The twin's teeth flashed in the darkness and she beckoned.

When the sentries were looking the other way, Fargo quietly rose. The moment he reached her, she threw her arms around his neck and kissed him hungrily on the mouth.

"It is my turn, handsome one."

"Blanche?" Fargo said.

"*Oui.* Who else? Jeanne already had her turn."

Fargo looped an arm around her waist and she giggled and snuggled closer, thinking he was going to ravish her. Instead, he swept her off her feet and carried her halfway into the gap and set her down.

"Ah. Yes. Here is nice," Blanche whispered in his ear. "No one can see us."

"Not so fast."

"What is the matter?" Blanche asked. "You did it with my sister. You must do it with me."

"You're not scared?"

"Of what? The attempts on your life?" Blanche smiled, and rubbed his leg. "Why should I be? They are out to kill you, not me."

"Thanks a heap," Fargo said.

"What would you have me do? Forgo my only chance? I have gone too long without as it is."

"And you want it, bad."

"Yes," Blanche said, and pressed herself to him.

Her hot lips scalded his mouth, his cheeks, his brow. Her hands were everywhere at once. She was twice the sensual firebrand her sister was.

For Fargo's part, that familiar tiny voice deep in his mind warned that he was being the biggest dunderhead this side of the divide. But he wanted to as much as she did.

Easing her down, he lay beside her.

"This is so exciting," Blanche whispered. "Maybe you'll be killed while we're doing it."

About to cup a breast, Fargo stared.

"Don't look at me like that. It would be something I'd remember the rest of my life."

Fargo almost changed his mind.

"My sister and I live for excitement," Blanche blathered on. "We crave it, like a starved man craves food. Otherwise, our lives would be dull and dreary. You've seen how we live. You've seen how our mother is."

Fargo went to put a finger to her lips, but she brushed his hand away.

"Don't be mad if the prospect of someone trying to kill you excites me. It's the same as making love when I'm not supposed to."

Fargo didn't see it that way. To silence her he kissed her. She tried to suck his tongue down her throat. Her fingernails dug into his shoulder while her other hand roved his chest. When he gripped her bottom she softly cooed deep in her throat.

The tramp of a foot stopped them.

Fargo looked up. A sentry was making a circuit over along the woods. The man was too far off to see or hear them.

He bent and Blanche gripped his chin in both hands and kissed him long and hard. She pried at his buckskin shirt, then at his belt, at his pants. The warm feel of her fingers as she slid them in sent a tingle up his back. The next moment she had hold of his pole.

"*Vous estas un etalon,*" Blanche breathed. She tugged to get his pants down.

Fargo helped by raising his hips. He didn't know what she had in mind and found out when her head dipped. For long minutes he drifted on velvet sensations of pure pleasure. Finally he pulled on her hair and she pushed his shirt up and lavished kisses on the muscles of his stomach and his ribs. He pulled again and their mouths locked.

He undid several ties and her robe parted. Sliding his hand underneath, he received a surprise; she was naked. Her breasts were as full and firm as her sister's, her belly as flat. He inhaled a nipple and nipped it and she shuddered. He inhaled the other and did the same and she bit his arm.

Fargo cupped both tits at once, and licked and sucked.

He ran the tip of his tongue from her cleavage to her navel and rimmed it. She had been liberal with her perfume, a musky fragrance that tantalized.

Blanche entwined her fingers in his hair and pulled so hard it was a wonder she didn't tear it out by the roots.

Placing a hand on her knee, Fargo caressed in slow circles until he was high on her thigh. A twist of his wrist and he was between them. She trembled as his finger parted her wet slit.

"Oh yes, handsome one," she whispered. "I want it so much."

She wasn't the only one. Fargo inserted a fingertip and she made a slight movement that drew all of his finger in. He added another, and pumped. Her back arched and for a moment he thought she'd cry out.

It occurred to Fargo how vulnerable he was. The killers could slay him without half trying. But he didn't stop. He stroked and kneaded and kissed and was himself stroked and caressed.

Blanche was the first to soar over the precipice. Her legs convulsively closed around his waist and she bucked like a mustang that refused to be ridden. But ride her he did, his hands on her hips to keep from being thrown. Wild with passion, she raked his back with her nails and drew drops of blood.

Fargo's own explosion occurred as she was slowing. With her bestowing tiny kisses on his throat and chest, he coasted to a sweaty stop and lay on top of her, panting.

"Goodness, that was nice," Blanche whispered.

Fargo grunted.

"Jeanne was right. You are sensational."

Closing his eyes, Fargo rolled off her. He could use eight hours of sleep. Instead, he commenced to put himself together, whispering, "You should go back in."

Blanche smiled and said dreamily, "I want to lie here awhile."

Fargo smacked her fanny, but not loudly. "I wasn't asking."

"Must you be so brusque?" Blanche complained. She sat up, pulled the robe around her, and tied the top tie. "Happy now?"

"I'll be happy when you're in the tent."

"I see. You are one of those who likes to be shed of the girl as soon as you can."

Fargo didn't waste his breath trying to explain that he didn't want her dead. He stood and offered his hand and pulled her to her feet. "Off you go," he said, and gave her another swat.

Pouting, Blanche hastened around the corner of the big tent.

Fargo walked into the open. The camp still lay peaceful under the sparkling stars. Two sentries were at the wagons, talking. Another was at the horses. He didn't see the fourth. He went to his bedroll and lay down and figured he would drift right off, but he felt restless. Half an hour crawled by and all he did was toss.

Finally deciding to hell with it, Fargo got up. He filled his tin cup and hunkered and was taking a swallow when a nearby sleeper cast off a blanket and sat up and swore. Grumbling, he jammed his hat on and got up and looked sleepily around.

It was Walker.

"The coffee's hot," Fargo said.

"Don't mind if I do," the Texan said. "I have to take a turn at standin' guard soon, anyway. So does my pard, Garret. That reminds me." He stepped to another sleeper and kicked him. "Rise and shine, you flea-ridden sack."

Garret swore.

Both Texans came over and Walker filled cups and gave one to his friend. "Have we missed much?"

Fargo thought of Blanche. "It's been quiet as can be."

Garret said, "I hope it stays that way."

"We can't wait to get back to town," Walker said. "We never should have hired on with these foreigners in the first place."

Garret nodded. "It's the last time I work for foreigners, that's for damn sure."

"It hasn't been that bad," Fargo said.

Walker blew on his coffee. "You must be forgettin' those Comanches."

"I tell you," Garret said, "I am worried sick they'll pay us another visit."

Fargo repeated his belief that the terrors of Texas wouldn't bother them again.

"What if you're wrong?" Walker said. "What if they reckon we have to pay for those you told us you killed?"

"Comanches ain't Christian no how," Garret said. "They don't forgive and forget. They get mad and they get even."

"I've been watching the horses," Fargo said. "If they caught Comanche scent, we'd know."

"Unless the red devils circle and come at us from downwind," Garret said. "Hell, a scout like you should know that."

Fargo sighed. He'd been on the lookout all day and seen no sign anywhere that Comanches were in the vicinity.

Garret wouldn't let it drop. "The thing with Comanches is you can't predict. They always do what you don't expect when you don't expect it."

"Some Texas Rangers told me once they'd rather fight anybody than Comanch," Walker said. "Apaches, banditos, you name it. And those Rangers are mighty tough hombres their own selves."

"That they are," Garret said. "If they're afraid of Comanches, we'd be fools not to be."

Fargo was tired of hearing about Comanches. "How soon do you have to stand guard?"

Garret opened his mouth to answer and the tip of an arrow burst out the center and sprayed blood in all directions.

26

Fargo threw himself to the ground and yelled, "Get down!" at Walker, who sat there gaping.

The arrow had come from past the tents.

Fargo glimpsed movement and was on his feet, the Henry in his hands. He zigzagged toward the woods, and another arrow streaked out but missed him by an arm's length or more.

Fargo covered the last ten yards and was in the trees.

It was black as pitch save for pale patches where the starlight filtered through.

He crouched, and an arrow buzzed well over his head and struck a tree.

The bowman, Fargo realized, wasn't much of an archer. He wondered if the arrow that killed Garret had been meant for him.

More movement caught his eye.

Whoever it was, they were fleeing.

Fargo rose and bounded in pursuit. He couldn't go as fast as he would like because of all the trees and undergrowth.

The figure looked back, the face a white patch in the blackness.

Fargo took a chance and ran full out. He was gaining when his foot caught on something and he pitched to his hands and knees. Pain shot up both legs and along his shoulders, but he was up and giving chase within a few heartbeats.

Fargo thought he knew who it was. That glimpse had been enough. He didn't know why the man was out to kill him, and he didn't care. The son of a bitch was as good as dead.

The killer was making enough racket to raise the dead, crashing through the brush with no attempt at stealth.

Good, Fargo thought. *Make it easier for me.*

The woods thinned and water shimmered darkly. They were at the river.

The figure came to the bank and launched himself into the Nueces.

Fargo reached the same spot and did likewise. He saw the man splashing madly for the other side, a bow in one hand, a quiver over his back. He came down with a loud splash of his own.

The water rose to his knees.

Fargo plowed through it like a mad bull. And he was mad as hell. He took it real personal when some son of a bitch tried to put him under.

The man slipped and stumbled, but he made it across and scrambled up the opposite bank. He glanced back again, and it pleased Fargo to detect fear in the twisted features.

He jerked the Henry up and hollered, "Hold it right there!"

The man reached the top of the bank.

Fargo was set to shoot him when his boot hit a slippery rock and his leg swept out from under him. Flailing his arm, he stayed upright. When he was steady enough to shoot, the man was gone.

Fargo churned out of the river and up the incline. He figured the man had kept running and he raced up over the bank—and there the killer was, another arrow notched to the string and the string pulled back to his cheek, set to fly. There was no time to dodge.

The bow twanged and the shaft shot through the short space between them—and struck Fargo's hat. He felt the arrow scrape his hair as his hat was lifted and whipped off. Fury seized him, and he swung the Henry's stock. The man flung the bow up to protect himself, and the blow shattered it.

Fargo slammed into him and they both went down.

"Bastard!" the man snarled, and pushed up wielding a dagger.

Fargo had lost hold of the Henry. He clawed for his Colt, only to discover it had fallen from his holster. Backpedaling, he bent and palmed the Arkansas toothpick.

"Come and get some," he taunted.

The man flashed a sneer and wagged his long blade. "I will enjoy this, American. I am not without skill."

"Brag comes easy," Fargo said. "But I've been to Missouri."

"I do not even know what that means."

"It means, Dupree, you have to show me," Fargo told him.

Claude Dupree's sneer widened. "Gladly," he said, and attacked.

Fargo sidestepped, blocked, feinted. Each move was countered. The Frenchman was worthless as an archer, but as a knife fighter he was deadly. They circled, stabbed, tested, taking each other's measure.

Claude's confidence grew. "You are the hardest person to kill," he said. "But now we have you."

"We?" Fargo said.

Angered by his mistake, Claude pounced. He speared the dagger at Fargo's throat, but Fargo skipped aside and retaliated with a thrust at Claude's side that Claude evaded.

Fargo had been in knife fights before. He'd learned never to talk, to concentrate on the other's blade and nothing else. It had become a rule with him, but he broke it when Claude sprang out of reach. "Why?" he said quickly. "What is this about?"

"You'll never know," Claude replied, tucking and moving the dagger in circles.

"Why Sifrein?" Fargo pressed. "Why the darts?"

"The darts were not just me."

"And the bow?" Fargo said, with a gesture at where it had fallen. "Was that to make everyone think the Comanches were to blame?"

"You think you are so smart," Claude said, and sprang.

Fargo retreated. Shifting, he cut at Claude's wrist, but Claude jerked his arm away. He slashed at Claude's throat, but again the Frenchman proved to be worthy of his boast.

The darkness was a factor. Fargo must be careful not to overextend. A simple mistake, any mistake, and the Frenchman would bury that dagger in his flesh.

They circled anew, Claude continuing to sneer.

A shout rose at the camp. It sounded like the count, yelling in French.

Claude gave a start, and straightened. "Damn you, American. Louis has gone into my tent and knows I am missing. He will figure it out."

"Figure what out?" Fargo said.

Instead of answering, Claude suddenly whirled and bolted.

Fargo went after him. In moments, though, he'd lost sight of where him. Stopping, he listened for footfalls but heard none.

Claude had stopped, too.

Boiling to end this once and for all, Fargo scoured every shape and shadow. There were so many, it was like trying to unravel a Stygian jigsaw. The polecat was there somewhere, but *where*?

A bush shook, and Fargo spun and was at it in long bounds. No one was behind it. He turned right and left. Again, nothing.

Fargo smothered a curse. Once again he was thwarted. He waited for Claude to move, but Dupree was too cagey.

More voices were raised across the river. Not just the count's. Henriette and Charles were calling for Claude, and the count and Philip and one of the twins were calling for him.

"Where are you?" The count's voice stood out. "What is going on?"

Fargo still didn't know. Why Claude wanted him dead was a mystery. It couldn't be over the few times they'd nearly come to blows. Or could it? he asked himself. Some men didn't take to being pushed around. He should know. He was one of them.

Vegetation crackled near the river, and Louis hollered, "Monsieur Fargo? Where are you?"

"This way!" Fargo answered. He saw no reason not to. Dupree knew where he was.

There was splashing and more crackling and snapping and the count appeared. He wasn't alone. Philip was at his side, and both had rifles.

"Here you are," Louis said in obvious relief. "I was worried."

"As was I," Philip said. "Monsieur Walker told us you went after a Comanche. And Claude is missing."

"Claude *is* the Comanche." Fargo enlightened them.

"How is that again?" the count asked.

Not taking his eyes off the vegetation, Fargo related how Claude had secretly taken a bow and quiver from a dead warrior and tried to kill him with it.

"But why?" Louis said. "What purpose would your death serve?"

"We find that out," Fargo said, "I can die a happy man."

"Eh?" Louis said. "Oh. American humor. But I am serious."

"You reckon I'm not?" Fargo rejoined.

Louis cupped a hand to his mouth. "Claude! Claude! Come out, do you hear?"

"I doubt he will, Father," Philip said.

"Let him hide if he wants," Fargo said. "In the morning we'll pull out and leave him."

"Strand him alone?" Louis said.

"But, monsieur," Philip declared, "that would not be humane."

"As if I give a damn," Fargo said. He'd as soon the bastard was torn apart by a bear or bit by a rattler.

"*Non*," Louis said. "I can't do that. We will stay until he shows himself."

Fargo wasn't going to stand there and debate it with Claude nearby. "We might as well head back."

Everyone was up: the family, the servants, the drivers, everyone.

"I don't believe it," Henriette said when the count informed her of Fargo's accusation. She was bundled in a heavy pink robe with a belt. "Claude would never do such a thing."

"I want the guards doubled," Louis commanded Philip. "See to it that—" He stopped. "Where is your brother? I don't see him anywhere."

Charles was missing. They called his name. One of the twins went into the big tent and shortly reappeared shaking her head.

"What in the world is going on?" Louis said.

"Torches," Henriette said. "Have the men bring torches and we will search for him."

"It can wait until morning," Fargo advised. "I'll track him down myself."

"No, you will not," Henriette said flatly. "I do not trust you."

At that juncture a driver ran up and snatched off his hat. "Pardon me, folks." He turned to Fargo. "I reckoned I should tell you."

"What now?" Fargo asked.

"It's Walker," the man said. "He heard you folks sayin' about that Claude feller killin' his pard, and he went off into the woods after him."

27

Fargo didn't get a lick of sleep. He drank half a pot of coffee and shortly before sunrise he ate a few pieces of jerky. That would have to do him. At the first blush of pink on the eastern horizon, he shouldered the Henry and headed for the wood. Halfway there he acquired a shadow. "What do you reckon you're doing?"

"Accompanying you," Philip said.

"It's better I go alone."

"My brother is out there. And my uncle, although I confess I do not care what fate befalls him. Mother insists either Father or I go with you, so I leave it to you. Which of us will it be?"

Fargo glanced back. Louis and Henriette and the twins were standing by the big tent. "You."

"I thought as much," Philip said, and smiled.

The ink of night was giving way to the gray veil of predawn. A few birds were astir, but the morning chorus had yet to commence.

Fargo moved with the assurance of a cougar, making no more noise than one of the large cats. Philip lacked his skill but did his best.

They came on some footprints, and stopped. The tracks weren't clear and they weren't complete, but they told Fargo which way the man had gone.

"Were these made by Charles?" Philip asked.

Fargo shook his head.

"My uncle, then?"

"You need to keep quiet," Fargo said. "And, no, these are Walker's tracks."

"How do you know?"

Fargo indicated the wedge made by the wide heel and how

the toes tapered. Charles and Claude both wore French foot-wear with small heels and square toes.

Philip was nervous and trying not to show it. Sweat caked his brow and occasionally a drop fell from his chin.

Fargo stuck to Walker's tracks. The Texan had roved all over the place, stopping often, no doubt to listen. Eventually the boot prints brought them to the Nueces. Walker had gone along it until he came to a gravel bar. Only a few yards separated the end of the bar from the other bank, and Walker had waded across.

The woods were thick. Briars were abundant. Rather than plunge through and be torn by thorns, Walker had gone around. It had slowed him and it slowed them.

The day was humid. Soon Fargo's buckskins clung to him like skin.

Thick woods loomed. The tracks showed that Walker's gait had changed. His long strides gave way to short steps. He'd seen or heard something, Fargo guessed, and cautiously stalked forward.

A small clearing materialized. In the center were the charred embers of a fire.

And Walker's body.

"Oh my," Philip said in dismay. *"Pas un autre."*

The Texan was on his back. He'd been facing the fire when he was slain, but there were no wounds on the front of his body.

Kneeling, Fargo rolled the body over. There, between the shoulder blades, was a blood-rimmed slit about two inches long.

Philip said, "He was struck from behind?"

Fargo nodded. "Someone stabbed him in the back."

"But who? My uncle Claude?"

Rising, Fargo went around the fire. Impressions in the dirt revealed the rest. "No. Your uncle was sitting here. Someone else stabbed him."

"But who?" Philip said again, and blinked. *"Non.* Not my brother?"

"Who else was out here?"

"Why would Charles help Claude? Are you suggesting they are in cahoots, as you Americans say?"

Fargo gestured at the dead Texan. "We have another saying. The proof is in the pudding."

"I don't know what to make of this," Philip said. "So much has happened, and there is little logic to any of it. Why would my uncle want you dead? It is insane."

Fargo stepped to Walker. "Uh-oh."

"What now?"

"His holster is empty." Fargo swore. "And I didn't think to ask his pard if he had a rifle."

"My uncle and Claude now have guns like yours, in other words."

It was unlikely the pair were still around, but Fargo crouched.

Philip imitated him. "Where can they have gotten to?" he whispered.

Two sets of tracks marked where Claude and Charles had circled to the river and forded the shallows.

On the other side Fargo paused. "Damn me for a fool."

"Why are you upset?" Philip studied the footprints. "*Mon Dieu*. I see. They point toward our camp." He broke into a run.

Fargo caught up as Philip was about to burst into the clearing. Lunging, he grabbed the younger man's arm and warned, "No!"

Philip swore and angrily tried to tug free. "Why are you—?" he began.

Putting a hand to his lips, Fargo pointed.

Bodies were everywhere; sprawled on their backs, sprawled on their bellies. The drivers and the other hired help lay scattered about the fires, most with tin cups in or near their outflung hands.

More bodies were in front of the big tent: every last servant, male and female, young and old, their expressions strangely peaceful, as if they were only asleep and having pleasant dreams. Near their hands were cups and glasses.

Not one of the bodies was moving.

Flies buzzed about, and when one landed on a maid's face, she didn't so much as twitch.

Philip was sheet-white. "What on earth?" he exclaimed in horror. Suddenly stiffening, he cried, "Where are my family?" Tearing his arm loose, he ran into the clearing.

"Damn it," Fargo said, and followed.

Philip raced to the big tent but stopped short. He seemed afraid to go in. He glanced at Fargo and his features hardened. He took a step, and abruptly halted.

The flap had parted. Out came Henriette. She was smiling and had a crystal glass in her hand. "Philip!" she said in delight. *"Où êtes-vous?"*

"Mother!" Philip declared in English, and motioned at the littered dead. "What has happened?"

"Everyone is getting their due."

"What?" Philip said. "Make sense, will you?" He tried to grab her hand, but she jerked back.

"S'il vous plait," Henriette said. "Control yourself." She held out the crystal glass. In it was an amber liquid. "Here. You must be thirsty after traipsing around in this terrible heat."

Philip took it. "Mother, how can you stand there smiling? Look around you. Everyone is dead."

"Not everyone," Henriette said. "You and I aren't. Now please. Obey your mother, and drink."

Absently, Philip started to raise the glass to his mouth.

Fargo had come up unnoticed. "Take one sip," he warned, "and you'll be as dead as the rest."

Henriette spun and her eyes danced with hate. "You. The man I hate most in this world." She turned back to her son. "Don't listen to him, Philip. He's a bumpkin. Drink and refresh yourself."

Philip peered into the glass at the amber liquid. He gazed about at the bodies. "My God," he said. He sniffed and asked, "What is this, Mother?"

"A tea I made," Henriette said. "It's quite delicious."

Fargo sidled around to Philip's side. "I bet they thought so," he said, with a nod at the servants lying like so much firewood.

"Stay out of this," Henriette said. "You'll be dealt with in a few moments." She touched her son's arm. "What are you waiting for? Drink."

"No, Mother," Philip said, and upended the glass over the grass. "Do you think me a simpleton?" He shook the empty glass at her. "You poisoned all these people, didn't you?"

"But of course," Henriette said cheerfully.

Philip took a step back as if she had hit him. "I must be losing my mind. Either that or you already have."

"Neither, dear boy," Henriette said. "They had to be killed, don't you see? After they have been scalped and mutilated, everyone will accuse the savages."

"Mother, what are you saying?"

Henriette sighed. "Honestly, Philip. You have always been slower than your brother, but this is ridiculous. Would you have me be blamed for the murders?"

Philip appeared close to tears. "You even killed our servants, many of whom have been with us for years."

"Use your head, son," Henriette said. "Why would the savages slay our drivers but not the staff? It would be too suspicious."

"Why murder anyone at all?"

"Perhaps it is just as well you are so slow between the ears. You wouldn't approve."

"*Approve?*" Philip cried. "Of *this*?"

"It is a means to an end, nothing more," Henriette said. "Who cares about the Americans? As for our servants, we can always hire new ones once we return to France."

"You *are* insane."

"If only everything had gone according to plan," Henriette said. "I wouldn't have had to trick them into toasting my dear, dead sister, and we wouldn't be having this talk."

"What plan, Mother?"

"Why, the plan to dispose of your father, of course," Henriette said.

Philip looked at Fargo in mute appeal.

"His coming to America was perfect," Henriette said. "There are so many ways a person may die here. When that buffalo charged us, I hoped it would spare us the trouble, but it didn't. So I went back to the original idea, with variations."

Philip touched his forehead. "This is almost more than I can bear. Why would you want Father dead? For his money?"

"Oh, please," Henriette said. "Louis let me have however much I wanted, and I was provided for in his will. No, money was never an issue."

"Then why?" Philip almost screamed.

"I did it for love."

Philip reeled as if drunk and had to try twice to talk. "Who are you in love with, if I may ask?"

Claude Dupree came around the tent with a rifle leveled. "That would be me."

28

Fargo went to raise the Henry, but a voice came from behind him.

"I wouldn't, American. Not unless you want me to blow a hole in you."

Fargo looked over his shoulder.

Charles had a rifle trained on him. The hammer was back and his finger was around the trigger. "Drop it."

Fargo did.

Philip glanced back, too, and his eyes welled with tears. "Brother? You are involved with this nightmare as well?"

"To a degree," Charles said, not taking his eyes off Fargo. "I'll let Mother explain."

Henriette gazed serenely about at the bodies, and smiled. "I propose we go in and sit at the table. There's no reason we can't be civilized about this."

"I disagree, my dear," Claude said. "We should kill the scout now."

"Nonsense. He is in our power. And after all the insults I've had to endure, I want to see his face when he learns the truth." Henriette laughed and took Philip's rifle from him. He made no attempt to resist.

"This one is too dangerous," Claude insisted, stepping toward Fargo.

"Disarm him, and hush," Henriette commanded.

Claude's jaw muscles twitched. "You heard her," he snapped. "Unbuckle your sidearm and let it fall. Slowly, or I will by God kill you anyway."

Using two fingers, Fargo undid the buckle. As the belt slid down his legs, he asked, "Where are the count and the twins?"

Philip stiffened. "That's right. Where are they, Mother? Don't tell me you've murdered them, too?"

Henriette held the tent flap open. "Come inside, son. All will be made clear."

Philip hesitated, then took a deep breath and went in.

"And now you, scout."

His hands out from his sides, Fargo entered. With two rifles at his back, he wasn't about to try anything. For the moment, anyway.

"*Père!*" Phillip cried, and ran to the long table.

At the far end sat Count Louis Tristan. He had been tied to the chair and gagged. There was a welt on his forehead and his cheek was split and bleeding. His head was slumped and his chest seemed to rise and fall with great effort.

Philip put a hand to his father's other cheek and tears rolled down his own. "What have you done to him, Mother?"

"Oh, Claude and I might have beat on him some," Henriette said. "I must confess that once I drew blood, I couldn't stop."

"Blanche and Jeanne?" Philip said. "What have you done with them?"

"They are in the back, tied up," Henriette revealed. "I've tried to persuade them to see my side of things, but they are being stubborn. They say that if I slay Louis and you, I must slay them, as well."

"Slay me?" Philip said, aghast.

"Naive as well as dumb," Henriette said. "Have a seat, both of you."

Fargo chose the chair at the other end before Philip could. He pulled it out farther than he needed to and eased down.

Claude Dupree moved a few yards to the other side of him.

Charles stayed near the flap.

"Now, then," Henriette said, walking around behind Louis and placing her hands on his shoulders. "Where to begin?"

"You can start with Claude fucking you," Fargo said.

Henriette's eyes glittered like ice. "Your crudity knows no limits. But yes, I suppose the place to start is with Claude and me falling in love."

Slumped in a chair, Philip raised his tear-streaked face. "Your sister's husband?"

"As the Italians would say, the thunderbolt strikes where it will," Henriette said. "It happened over a course of years. I grew more and more dissatisfied with your father. To be frank, he wasn't much in bed, not in these later years, anyway. And I grew increasingly unhappy, that I was given so little say in the management of our estates."

"So you slept with Claude," Philip said in disgust. He glared at his uncle. "And you cheated on Aunt Odette."

"The woman was a cow," Claude said.

"Have a care," Henriette said to him. "She was my sister, after all."

"Get on with your damn story," Fargo broke in, and leaned back in his chair so that the front legs rose off the ground. His feet planted firm to keep his balance, he lowered his right arm to his boot.

"Must you always be *barbare*?" Henriette chided. "But, yes, we should get this over with so that Claude and I can prepare to return to Corpus Christi and report the massacre by the savages."

"It won't wash, lady," Fargo said. "The army will know it wasn't the Comanches."

"*Au contraire*," Henriette said. "Claude there has some of their arrows left. And he saved a few other weapons of theirs, as well. We will scatter them about, and he will lift a few scalps. That should suffice to convince the authorities, *non*?"

The hell of it was, Fargo reflected, it just might work. "Was it your idea to poison all those people out there?"

"*Oui*," Henriette said. "With the pygmy poison I obtained in Africa. I'm afraid I had to use the last of it in my special tea."

Fargo noticed a pouch hanging from Claude's belt, and a blowgun tucked under the belt next to it. But he didn't let on.

"Oh, Mother," Philip said forlornly.

"Grow up," Henriette snapped. She touched a fingernail to her chin. "Now where was I? Ah yes. It was when your father announced we were going to Africa that I decided I'd endured enough. I told him, repeatedly, I had no interest in going. I reminded him, again and again, how dangerous it was, and that he was putting our lives and the lives of our children in peril. But would he listen? No. Would he change his mind? No. How ironic."

"Ironic?" Philip said.

"Yes, dear. It was in Africa that the idea first came to me that I would be better off with him dead. No more skulking around

153

to be with Claude. Better yet, with me his widow, most of the family fortune would fall into my hands."

"All this to satisfy your greed and your lust," Philip said.

"And get this, my son," Henriette went on blithely, oblivious of his remark. "The moment it came to me was when we saw that pygmy kill a monkey with his blowgun. Remember?"

"Yes, Mother, I remember."

"It took a lot of persuasion for me to convince their chief to let me have one. I had to let him look up my skirts."

"Mother!"

"Oh, I didn't let him touch me or anything. He was curious about white women, whether we were different than pygmy women." Henriette laughed merrily. "It was quite comical."

Philip deflated and hung his head. "That I should live to hear all this."

"You really need to grow up," Henriette said.

"So what now, Mother? Do you finish off Father and kill Monsieur Fargo and myself and have that pig Claude strangle my sweet sisters?"

Claude colored and pointed his rifle at Philip. "Here, now, boy. Have a care."

"Don't you dare shoot him," Henriette warned. "He's my son and I will deal with him."

Fargo raised his left hand. His right was next to his boot. "I have a question."

"Eh?" Henriette said, and frowned. "So long as you're not crude, you may ask it."

"How about Charlie here?"

"What?" Henriette said.

"What?" Charles echoed.

Fargo began to slip his fingers into his boot. "Where does he fit in?"

"Oh." Henriette coughed. "He caught Claude and me together one night and was going to tell Louis, but I prevailed on him to keep silent in return for his brother's share of the inheritance."

Philip's head snapped up. "Oh, Mother. Is there no end to your evil?"

"Does Charlie get to go on breathing after it's all over?" Fargo stalled.

"Why wouldn't he?" Henriette rejoined.

"He knows everything," Fargo said. "He could testify against you. Put you and your lover behind bars for the rest of your lives."

"Charles would never do such a thing."

Claude, though, was staring at the oldest son and gnawing on his lip.

"If it was me," Fargo said, "I wouldn't want witnesses."

"What are you up to?" Henriette asked.

Claude turned slightly so that now his rifle was pointed at Charles. "Perhaps the American is right, my darling. Perhaps we should make a clean sweep of it. The girls. Philip." He nodded at Charles. "All of them."

"See here, now," Charles said. "I've kept quiet all this time, haven't I? Doesn't that prove I can be trusted?"

Fargo wrapped his fingers around the Arkansas toothpick. He leaned back a little more and balanced on the balls of his boots.

"It proves nothing," Claude Dupree was saying. "You might change your mind a year from now. Or five years."

Henriette came out of her chair. "Claude, you stop this, do you hear? I vouch for Charles. I trust that he will keep his word."

"You're his mother," Claude said.

Fargo tried to catch Philip's eye, but Philip was staring morosely down.

"Don't you see what the scout has done?" Henriette asked. "He's turned you against us, the clever bastard."

At last Philip looked in Fargo's direction. Fargo flicked his eyes at Claude and then at Charles and nodded at Philip.

Philip's brow puckered. He started to smile, and nodded back.

It caught Henriette's attention. "What are you smiling about?" she asked suspiciously.

"I can answer that," Fargo said. "They have another saying in Texas. Maybe you've heard of it."

"What are you talking about?"

"The time has come," Fargo said, "to root hog or die."

29

Fargo came up out of the chair and flung himself at Claude Dupree. Claude tried to swivel the rifle at him, but Fargo swatted the barrel aside and stabbed the toothpick at Claude's chest. The blade struck a rib bone and glanced off.

Fargo grabbed the barrel. He heard Henriette yell something and a bellow from Charles and then the boom of a shot.

Claude was swearing furiously in French. He wrenched on the rifle, and when Fargo held on, he aimed a vicious kick at Fargo's knee. Fargo sidestepped. He thrust his leg out and pulled on the barrel in a bid to trip Claude, but Dupree leaped over his leg.

Fargo glimpsed Philip struggling with Charles for Charles's rifle.

Henriette had come around the table and was shrieking at her oldest to kill her youngest.

Pain exploded in Fargo's chin. Claude had punched him. He speared the toothpick at Claude's throat, but Claude seized his wrist. Grappling furiously, they stumbled this way and that.

Fargo was surprised at the Frenchman's strength. He shifted to avoid a knee to the groin and retaliated with the same, only to have Claude take the blow on his thigh.

"I will kill you, American!" Claude hissed, spittle flecking his mouth. His eyes practically bulged from their sockets, he was so enraged.

In their twisting and grappling they ended up near the flap.

Suddenly Claude did the last thing Fargo expected; he let go of the rifle and Fargo's wrist, whirled, and bolted from the tent.

Fargo went to go after him and heard Philip cry out in pain. He stopped and turned.

Philip was on the ground, grimacing in agony, his hand to his side. Bright scarlet flowed from between his spread fingers.

Henriette stood over him, a knife clutched in her hand, blood dripping from the blade she had buried.

Charles was staring at her in both horror at what she had done and relief that she had come to his aid. "*Merci, ma mère.*"

Henriette looked at Philip. She cackled and bent. "Did you think I would let you spoil everything, stupid one? After all the trouble I've gone to? The years of waiting and plotting?"

"Mother . . ." Philip gasped.

"You were always the weakest," Henriette said. "Even your sisters are stronger than you."

Philip groaned and raised his hand and stared at the blood. "How could you?"

"I will do anything to acquire what I desire," Henriette said, "and I desire Claude. He is much more endowed than your father."

"Mother!" Charles cried.

By then Fargo had the toothpick under his belt and was raising Claude's rifle to his shoulder.

"You never truly loved us," Philip said. "Not if you can do this."

"I do it because I'm stronger than you," Henriette boasted. "Because I do what I need to, no matter the consequences."

"You gave birth to me."

"Much to my regret. Were you half the man you should be, you would side with me in this."

"Rot in hell, Mother," Philip said.

Henriette raised the knife in both her hands. "Time to end your useless life."

"Henriette?" Fargo said softly. She looked over at him and he shot her between the eyes.

For a few moments the tableau froze.

Then Fargo spun toward Charles, but the older son darted into a passage that led to the back.

"Go after him!" Philip urged. "I will be all right."

Fargo glanced out the tent. Claude wasn't anywhere in sight. "Keep an eye out for your uncle," he said, and flew after Charles.

The tent was divided into sections partitioned by canvas walls, and each section had an individual flap. The first flap he came out was tied back and no one was there.

The same with the second.

The flap to the third section was shut. From the other side came a whimper.

"I know you're in there," Fargo said.

"Have a care, American," Charles growled. "Look in here and see what I mean."

Fargo cautiously opened the flap.

Blanche and Jeanne were on their knees, facing him. They were bound, wrists and ankles, and gagged. Both their faces were bruised and gashed. They stared up at him through tear-filled eyes, the twin on the right trying to speak through her gag.

Behind them, his rifle pressed to the head of the one on the left, stood Charles. "One wrong move and your lovers die."

Fargo stayed still.

"That's right, American," Charles said. "I know about you and my charming sisters. I spied on them when they were with you."

"You spy on people a lot."

Charles grinned and shrugged. "We all have our secret pleasures." He paused. "My mother is dead, isn't she?"

"Dead as hell," Fargo said.

"And Claude?"

"He ran off."

Charles muttered in French, then said, "I'm not surprised. He has no backbone, that one. Except for seducing women, he has little talent at all."

"Yet you helped him and your mother."

"For my brother's share of the inheritance," Charles said, and laughed. "Have you any idea how much that will be? My father was most generous to all of us."

"But not generous enough to suit you."

"What can I say?" Charles said, and shrugged again. "I should thank you, though. With my mother gone, I am next in line. All I have to do is dispose of these two and my simpleminded brother and I inherit everything."

"What about Claude?"

"What about him?" Charles rejoined. "He is nothing to me. I'm better off with him dead, too. Then there is no one who can testify against me." He chortled. "I will be smarter at this than Mother. She and Claude hired Sifrein to dispose of you because they were worried you would interfere with their plans for my father. I won't make their mistake. I won't hire anyone. I will do it all myself."

While he'd jabbered, Fargo looked at the twins and then at

Charles. The twin on the right nodded and nudged the twin on the left.

"Set down that rifle where I can see it," Charles commanded. "Try to use it and I squeeze the trigger."

Using his left hand, Fargo slowly placed the rifle on the ground. His right hand was slightly behind his pant leg, the toothpick's hilt tight in his palm.

"*Excellente*," Charles said, and raised the muzzle of his rifle. "You've made it ridiculously easy."

"Whenever you're ready."

"Are you talking to me?" Charles asked.

"No," Fargo said.

The twin on the right turned and rammed her head and shoulders at Charles's shins. The twin on the left twisted and levered her head higher.

Charles swore and sprang back, but he wasn't quick enough. Staggering, he almost fell. He kicked at the twin on the left, then seemed to remember Fargo was there, and turned.

It was like driving a hot knife into butter. The doubled-edged steel caught Charles in the small hollow at the base of his throat and went in all the way to the hilt.

Fargo held it there, and smiled.

Charles tried to speak. Warm blood gushed, spilling down the front of his shirt.

"This is for your father," Fargo said, and twisted the toothpick, hard. "This is for your brother." He twisted it the other way. "And this," he said, "is for me." And he cut at an angle, opening the throat clear to the jawbone. Jerking the toothpick out, he stepped back.

Charles crashed to earth. He convulsed, groaned, and died.

Quickly stooping, Fargo cut at the rope on the wrists of the twin on the right. "Philip is out front with your pa," he said as he sliced. "Free your sister and help them."

"Where will you be?"

"Claude," Fargo said, and let it go at that. He raced out but slowed as he neared the opening in case Dupree was waiting out there with the blowgun. Warily poking his head out, he saw nothing but bodies.

Fargo slid the toothpick into its ankle sheath to free his hands. In a few strides he was at his gun belt and snatched up the Colt. He pivoted to one side and then to the other, but no Claude.

Fargo strapped on his gun belt, jammed the Colt in the holster, and bent to pick up the Henry.

"Leave it where it is," Claude said, stepping from the gap between the tents. He had the blowgun close to his lips.

Fargo froze.

"All I do is puff and you are dead," Claude gloated.

"Charles told me you're yellow," Fargo said. "I figured you had run off."

"He is a fine one to talk," Claude said, coming closer, the blowgun poised.

"He won't be doing any talking," Fargo said, "unless it's in hell."

"There is only me, then?" Claude said, taking another step. "I will deal with the girls and the others after I have taken care of you."

"You should have grabbed a gun and shot me."

"Non," Claude said. "I like this better." He ran his hand along the blowgun. "So smooth, and so deadly."

"Do you think you can put one of those darts in me before I reach you?"

Charles smirked and took another step. "As close as I am? But of course."

"Try," Fargo said, and threw himself through the air.

He slammed his fist into Claude's gut just as Claude pressed the blowgun to his lips.

Dupree uttered a gurgling cry and a gasp, and tottered. He caught himself, his eyes widening in horror, and clutched at his throat. Doubling over, he broke into a violent coughing spasm that ended with him on his side in the dirt.

"The thing with blowguns," Fargo said, "is that the dart can come out either end."

Claude hacked. He wheezed. He dug his nails into his neck. *"Non!"* he wailed. He shuddered, screamed, and was no more.

Fargo drew back a boot to kick the bastard, just for the hell of it, but lowered his foot. There were people in the tent who needed help, and two of them might need comforting on the way to Corpus Christi.

Fargo smiled.

LOOKING FORWARD!
The following is the opening section of the next novel in the exciting *Trailsman* series from Signet:

TRAILSMAN #368
COLORADO CROSSHAIRS

Buckskin Joe, Colorado (Nebraska Territory), 1860—where a gold camp spawns more murder than wealth, and Fargo proves there's high assay in lead.

"Whoopee ti yi yo!" shouted Steve Holman, startling his horse. "Gonna get rich, Dave! Soon that pretty wife of yours will be decked out in fancy feathers. No more hog and hominy on *our* plates, mister."

"Hush down, you fool," Dave warned his younger brother. "This ain't Fiddler's Green."

About fifty yards out ahead of them on the steep mountain trace, a tall man in fringed buckskins wheeled his black-and-white pinto stallion around and rode back to join them. A broad black plainsman's hat left half of his crop-bearded face in shadow. He was lanky and his muscle-corded body hard as sacked salt.

Fargo said, "Jess, I've—"

"That's Steve," Dave corrected him. "Jess stayed with the women."

Fargo cursed mildly under his breath. Telling the identical Holman twins apart was dealing him misery. "All right, Steve it is, then. By any name, son, you can't get rich unless you stay alive. And hog-calling in the middle of Mountain Ute country is a good way to get your life over in a puffin' hurry."

"Hell, Mr. Fargo, you yourself said they already know we're up here."

Fargo cast a patient glance at the young pilgrim. Steve Holman's face was raw from wind and rough soap, beardless, without even one deep sun crinkle yet. But he had the strong jaw and direct, alert gaze of a man determined to watch and learn. Fargo knew that both the twins were green, piss-proud, and full of sass, but he had liked them instantly.

"Sure as cats fighting they know we're up here," he replied. "But I'd appreciate some warning before they attack, and how can we hear anything with you bellowing like a castrated bull?"

Dave Holman nodded agreement even as he carefully guided an Owensboro freight wagon down the steep northern slope of Yellow Grizz Mountain. He and Fargo had rigged the wagon with Mormon brakes, a tree lashed to the back to slow the downhill descent.

"Fargo's right," he said. "The Utes know we're up here. But I think they figure us for soft-brains. What kind of crazy-by-thunder son of a bitch cuts out blocks of ice and stores them, then hauls them off the mountain?"

Fargo grinned, riding beside the wagon. His vigilant, sun-creased eyes left nothing alone. "That's good if they think we're crazy. Crazy white men scare them sick and silly, and it's heap big bad medicine to kill one. But I wouldn't assume you're safe, Dave. You were a frontier soldier and you know the red man is notional."

Two weeks earlier Fargo, finding himself light in the pockets, had hired on as a scout and guard for the Rocky Mountain Ice Company, owned by Holman and his green-antlered twin brothers. They harvested blocks of winter ice from Lake Bridger and stored them, packed in sawdust, in the earthen ice-house they had built. Now that warm weather had set in, they were making a king's ransom hauling ice in their big, lumbering wagon to the mushrooming mining camps below. In wide-open places like Kellyville, California Gulch, and Buckskin Joe, ice was a luxury almost worth its weight in gold.

As if reading Fargo's thoughts, Dave said, "Steve and Jess keep harping on how we're rich. But you spoke God's truth, Fargo. Nothing's cheaper than an Indian haircut."

"We *are* rich," Steve insisted. "We'll haul in two hundred dollars for this one load alone. Riley's grog shop in Buckskin Joe can fetch *two dollars* for a glass of iced beer. Mister, this frozen water beats any crop we ever sold back in Iowa."

Dave waved this off. "Rich? Sell your ass, brother. Right now we're just a cocklebur outfit. Not only that, we're squatters up on top this mountain."

"So is every sourdough down below who filed him a claim. Ain't nobody driving them off, right, Mr. Fargo?"

"They won't have to be driven off, Steve. The gold nuggets will play out quicker than scat. I've been in gold camps in the Sierra, on the Comstock, in the Snake River country, and all over the Rockies. It's the same anthem everywhere: cash in and move on. Today iced beer sells at twenty times the going rate back in the States. Tomorrow the diggings and grog shops have pulled up stakes. And there goes your ice trade."

Steve looked glum at this intelligence. Then his face perked up. "But it could last long enough for us to salt away a small fortune, huh?"

Fargo only nodded absently, busy studying their surroundings. The newborn sun was balanced like a brass coin above the grassy foothills to the east, making them resemble a dark pod of whales. Yellow Grizz Mountain was the highest peak in the Park Range of the Rockies, situated between the South Platte and the Arkansas rivers. Its slopes were dotted with bluebonnets and daisies and splashes of bright red Indian paintbrush.

However, Fargo wasn't swayed by the natural beauty. For, unfortunately, this slope, the only way down to the gold-bearing creeks, was also a dry-gulcher's paradise. Huge tumbles of boulders flanked the ancient trace, interspersed with thick stands of jack pine and hawthorn bushes.

"Trouble?" Dave asked him.

"I don't see any," Fargo replied, not bothering to add *but I sure's hell sense it.*

"If Mr. Fargo don't see it," Steve blustered, "then it ain't there. Why, I read in *Leslie's Weekly* how he can follow a wood tick on solid rock."

"Newspaper bunkum," Fargo said in his mild way. "Now, why the hell would a man want to follow a wood tick?"

It was heel-fly time, and as the party traveled lower the ovaro began to snort in irritation. That bothered Fargo—he depended on the stallion's keen senses, and a pesky distraction like flies could weaken them.

"You ask me," Dave said, "the real trouble is down below, not up here. Especially in Buckskin Joe."

Even the ebullient Steve, ever one to find the silver lining, nodded at this, scowling. "That shines, Brother Dave. That bunch in camp really gripe my ass. They call us fodder forkers and hay slayers and punkin rollers. If we hadn't hired on Mr. Fargo, we'd be as cold as this ice by now."

"Now you're whistling, brother," Dave agreed, carefully riding the brake with his left foot to help the team. "The crap sheets are right about one thing. Any man past the hundredth meridian is either on the dodge or seeking pay dirt."

Fargo grunted at this. "Or both. I'd say one in five of those jaspers in Buckskin Joe are killers. First time I rode in and met you two, I recognized at least ten of them by name."

"When we first got here," Dave said, "it was just a few sourdoughs in brush shanties, some of them not even armed. Now there's a new breed moving in—hard cases with shifty eyes and tied-down guns. You won't see 'em panning the creeks, neither."

Fargo nodded. "Mostly Missouri trash. Day before yesterday I spotted Gus Latimer."

"Who's he?" Steve demanded.

Dave's sunburned face creased in a frown. "They say Latimer can draw quicker'n you can spit and holler howdy."

Steve looked at Fargo. "Is that the straight?"

Fargo nodded. "He's from Blue Springs, Missouri, the cradle of killers. One of the West's most feared draw-shoot artists. I've spotted him a few times and had no trouble with him, but he's savage as a meat axe. And he's not particular about whether the bullets are in the front or back."

"He's also a hired jobber," Dave chimed in. "He didn't just drift in on his own. He's generally doing dirt work for the cod-fish aristocracy."

Fargo grunted affirmation. "He's here to help some rich toff acquire claims—one way or another."

"Well, these easy-money lemmings won't want our operation," Steve opined. "We're way up the mountain, and besides, it's backbreaking labor to harvest and haul ice."

Fargo agreed with the kid on that point. But the ovaro suddenly bridled, whiplashing his head up.

"Steady on, boys," Fargo warned. "Might be trouble on the spit. Swing your weapons to the ready."

Steve slid a Greener twelve-gauge from his saddle boot, an excellent piece for close-in defense. Dave left his Army-issue Colt revolver in its flap holster and grabbed his Spencer carbine. Fargo tugged the sixteen-shot brass-frame Henry from its saddle scabbard and levered a cartridge into the breech.

"Utes?" Dave said in a low voice.

Fargo said nothing, carefully scanning the terrain on both sides of them. The ovaro bridled again and he realized it was flies tormenting him. Fargo leaned forward to shoo them off with his hat.

"Nasty hatch this year," he remarked as he gigged the stallion forward.

"Damn things are giving Inez conniption fits," Dave said, meaning his pretty, young wife. "That's one reason she's been scratchin' at you lately, Skye."

"Man alive, she's a she-grizz when Mr. Fargo comes around," Steve agreed. "She figures he's a killer, I reckon. Then again, he is."

Fargo grinned. He was still digesting a snug breakfast of eggs, slapjacks and ham-doin's. "She sets out good grub, boys, so let her scratch. My hide is thick."

Every man had his obsession, and Dave Holman's was his wife. "Her mama taught her to hitch her wagon to a star. Looks like she hitched it to an army mule."

"You're the world-beatingest man, Dave," Steve pitched in when Fargo said nothing. "Always talking yourself down on account of that woman. Hell, you've built up an icehouse and a vegetable business, all on one stick. You'd ought to feel proud."

"That ain't good enough for Inez, little brother, and you know it. It's trade, and she favors somethin' more genteel. Somethin' where I just make the money without handling it."

"Huh," was all Steve said, spitting into the wind and getting it all over his shirt. Fargo grinned at the ignorant kid and shook his head.

But it was Fargo's opinion on women that Dave valued, considering him a worldwide expert on the subject. He waited until he caught the Trailsman's eye and said, "Oh, I know she acts like an F.F.V. sometimes—you know, the first families of Virginia? But she's just a pretty Buckeye from Dayton with a schoolteacher daddy and a ma who took in sewing."

Dave was waiting expectantly, so Fargo reluctantly answered. "You can't rightly blame a woman out West for putting on airs. It's a mean, hardscrabble life and chips away at their spirit. They can't hardly lay hands on a bright bit of cloth, and the only book around is likely a Bible or a gun catalog."

"Don't it beat the Dutch?" Dave plowed on as if Fargo hadn't spoken. "She don't like me to cut shines nor smoke tobacco nor get oiled. No gambling, no cussing, and get this—no fofaraw on Sunday! Hell, that's the only day I'm rested enough for it."

"It makes sense that she'd object," Fargo replied from a deadpan. "After all, seven days makes a hole weak."

All three men enjoyed a hearty laugh at the bawdy pun.

"Speaking of fofaraw," Steve put in, "that's one thing I do miss since we left Iowa—women. Them strumpets down in the camps all got the French pox."

"Pipe down and ready your weapons," Fargo said tersely as the ovaro began to stutter-step nervously toward the right-hand side of the trace. "It ain't flies this time. Eyes left!"

In a heartbeat things started happening nineteen to the dozen. A hideous, yipping war cry broke out from the jack pines on their left. One moment Steve sat his saddle, pivoting to aim his Greener. An eyeblink later the earth seemed to swallow him up. *Fwipping* arrows rained in on Fargo, spinning his hat off his head. The sudden shrieking panicked the wagon team, and they tore off down the mountainside at a breakneck pace, bouncing Dave off the board seat and onto the trail.

"Put at 'em!" Fargo roared to Dave, bringing his Henry up into the offhand position. But it was impossible to draw a bead: There wasn't an Indian in sight.

No other series packs this much heat!

THE TRAILSMAN

#340: HANNIBAL RISING
#341: SIERRA SIX-GUNS
#342: ROCKY MOUNTAIN REVENGE
#343: TEXAS HELLIONS
#344: SIX-GUN GALLOWS
#345: SOUTH PASS SNAKE PIT
#346: ARKANSAS AMBUSH
#347: DAKOTA DEATH TRAP
#348: BACKWOODS BRAWL
#349: NEW MEXICO GUN-DOWN
#350: HIGH COUNTRY HORROR
#351: TERROR TOWN
352: TEXAS TANGLE
#353: BITTERROOT BULLETS
#354: NEVADA NIGHT RIDERS
#355: TEXAS GUNRUNNERS
#356: GRIZZLY FURY
#357: STAGECOACH SIDEWINDERS
#358: SIX-GUN VENDETTA
#359: PLATTE RIVER GAUNTLET
#360: TEXAS LEAD SLINGERS
#361: UTAH DEADLY DOUBLE
#362: RANGE WAR
#363: DEATH DEVIL
#364: ROCKY MOUNTAIN RUCKUS
#365: HIGH COUNTRY GREED
#366: MOUNTAINS OF NO RETURN

**Follow the trail of Penguin's Action Westerns at
penguin.com/actionwesterns**